"I wanted to
first time I sa

Laurel just stared a

"You want to be a bad girl, Laurel?"

She gasped and said softly, "Yes."

"How? Tell me."

But Laurel was silent. Instead, her hands moved reflexively over his bare biceps, along his back to his buttocks.

Removing her ruined blouse, Mac dropped it onto the floor. Seconds later, her bra followed. With a warm wet mouth he suckled one breast, and with his free hand he stroked the other.

When Laurel arched into him, her hands going around his neck, he pulled away, asking raggedly, "Tell me how you want it, Laurel, so I know." But he already knew. He'd seen her answer in print.

"Hard and rough, Mac. Hard and rough."

Their eyes connected, and for one brief instant he thought she regretted the words. But in his heart he knew otherwise. So he took her then and didn't let go till morning.

Dear Reader,

The first bad boy I ever fell in love with was Han Solo. Oh yes, that cocky grin, that elusive "catch me" challenge, those bedroom eyes. Who could resist? Certainly not even tough cookie Princess Leia. That's because a bad boy is a dreamer, a seducer, a daredevil. He is a man of mystery and a fascinating paradox.

What happens when Laurel Malone falls for Theodore Macallister Tolliver III's bad-boy deception and discovers that he isn't the kind of man she wants? Or is he? Join Laurel as she is irresistibly drawn to the man she thinks is her Prince Charming and finds herself in love with the frog instead.

I thank you for taking the time to read my book, and hope it brings you a lot of enjoyment. Let me know. Drop me a line care of Harlequin Books, 225 Duncan Mill Road, Don Mills, Ontario M3B 3K9, Canada or visit www.karenanders.com

Best!

Karen Anders

MANHANDLING

by

Karen Anders

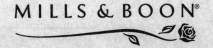

To Vernell Johnson for her steadfast friendship,
the definition of the term "Baby Got Back"
and the hysterical laughter. You go, girl!

First published in Great Britain 2005
by Harlequin Mills & Boon Limited,
Eton House, 18-24 Paradise Road, Richmond, Surrey TW9 1SR

© Karen Alarie 2004

ISBN 0 263 84462 5

14-0705

Printed and bound in Spain
by Litografia Rosés S.A., Barcelona

1

Pour the honey on him. Let it flow across his chest, down over his washboard abs and pool in his naval. Lap it up with your tongue and taste the golden sweetness. Stroking is an erotic sensation sure to give him slow, muscle-melting pleasure. Honey is the nectar of the gods, the food of love, apply generously and go slooow....

"Miss Malone, I'm afraid your father is going to be delayed. He apologizes." Laurel Malone's father's secretary, Lucy Sheridan, stood at the large double doors of her father's office, her lips pinched, and her eyes cold.

Laurel dropped the copy of *SPICE* magazine into her lap, the article describing the uses of aphrodisiacs to enhance sex forgotten. Chilled by the blunt, unfeeling sound of Lucy's voice, a voice that could wilt a flower like a killing frost, Laurel shifted. Lucy was just one more unpleasant aspect of her father's multimillion dollar Wall Street brokerage house, a longtime fixture in upper Manhattan. She hated this place. This empty, dead place where people moved around like automatons.

With an irritable flick of her wrist, she sent the ends of her long black hair over her shoulder.

She closed her eyes to collect her composure. She'd specifically asked her father to lunch, so that she could talk to him about her mother's memorial and his lack of interest in it.

Anne Wilks Malone had been a driving force behind the large art deco collection that now was on exhibition at the Metropolitan Museum of Art. To honor her mother, Laurel had come up with the idea of holding an auction in her mother's name and donate the proceeds to the Met. It seemed a fitting way to celebrate her mother's anniversary.

The auction would be held two short weeks from now and they had lost their room at Christie's. The New York auction house had doubled-booked and so they were out of a place to host their event.

She needed his help and advice, but every time she'd tried to talk to him, he put her off or sidestepped the discussion. He couldn't possibly be avoiding the subject—no, that couldn't be it. He'd worshipped her mother and would want an update as to the progress of the preparations for the charity auction of art deco pieces.

With a practiced voice devoid of annoyance, she replied. "That's fine. I'll wait."

Her father's very efficient personal assistant nodded and closed the heavy oak door to her father's plush office.

Anticipating her father's somewhat unpredictable schedule, she'd brought the latest issue of *SPICE* magazine.

Laurel tried to focus on the words, but decided to wait and read the rest of the article at home later in a more comfortable environment. Contemplating what she could do to a man with honey was best done in private.

The auction and her father's reluctance to help weren't the only things on her mind. Annoyance snapped through her like currents of dangerous electricity.

She grabbed up the magazine and turned the pages with short, choppy movements.

Calm, cool, collected, she heard her mother's soft voice in her head. *A lady always acts professional.*

But Laurel couldn't help her anger, even as she slowed her movements and tried to, at least, act calm. She'd only been a senior analyst at Waterford Scott for one month and now Mr. Herman was making noises about taking the Spegelman account away and giving it to Mark Dalton, the once pleasant Mark Dalton who now looked at her like she was a sneaky backstabber.

She couldn't understand why he was getting the big account. Mr. Herman's excuse was that her job needed to be pared down so that she could focus on her other more demanding clients, but it didn't ring true for Laurel. She was on the fast track to make partner, and she couldn't see how taking a big client away from her was going to make her a better analyst. It didn't make sense to her.

She closed her eyes and took a deep breath. Worrying about it now would only give her heartburn. Let it go, she told herself as she looked down at her open magazine. Her sister-in-law Haley, editor of *SPICE,* sure knew how to pick the men she showcased in her magazine. In advance of the quickly approaching summer, this issue had numerous guys sprawled in the sand,

over a surfboard, and one fine example standing underneath an outside shower. Hoo boy!

She'd been working long hours ever since she'd gotten the promotion. It had been too long since she'd felt
the wonderful touch of a man's mouth moving oh-so-
slowly across her aching flesh. Too long since she'd felt
the exquisite weight and warmth of a hard body covering hers, the sleek stroke and special friction of a man
sliding deep in a grinding rhythm. No sex toy could du-
plicate those wonderful, erotic sensations. She longed
for a carnal link with a real-live man.

Another bone of contention with her father. He was
very vocal about the kind of men she dated. Even
though she was twenty-eight years old, her father continued to try to control her life and, for the most part,
Laurel let him. His influence had increased since her
mother had died a year ago.

She did value his advice and knew that he had her
best interests at heart. So she'd caved when he thought
that accounting would suit her. She'd also caved in accepting the lucrative job at Waterford Scott, one of the
big five accounting firms in the United States.

She had had her little rebellions, too, such as, the
SoHo brownstone when he wanted her in upper
Manhattan in one of the posh neighborhoods, and her
refusal when he offered to manage her mother's trust.

Her father wanted her to settle down and get married to a respectable, normal guy. It's not that Laurel
didn't want that, she did. It was her father's determi-
nation that the guy be someone who worked in this
mausoleum—boring, unappealing, and dedicated to
fulfilling all her father's wishes, that irked her. She

wanted a man who'd stand up to her father and fulfill all *her* wishes. Her father's will was formidable and she suspected she'd end up with exactly the kind of guy her father wanted for her. Then her life would be drab and staid just like his office.

She sighed. She was being overdramatic today and shook off the mood. She continued to flip through the pages until she came across the section that usually showcased the *SPICE* quiz. A little frisson of excitement sizzled through her.

The title read *Who's Your Hottie? Some women prefer a man in uniform, others a man straddling a Harley. What kind of man turns you on? Take the* SPICE *quiz and see who lights your fire.* Laurel looked at her watch and then down at the quiz. Her father would probably be at least another fifteen minutes, and she wasn't going to stew about losing an important client until it actually happened. Besides, it would be fun to see who she might enjoy spending some carnal time with.

Hah. What a word. Carnal: knowledge of a physical and especially sexual nature. Carnal desire. But it also meant a worldly or earthly carnality. Neither meaning fit her at all. She had lived her life exactly as she was supposed, perfect daughter, perfect debutante, perfect corporate ladder-climber.

She had always been so *darn* good.

Maybe it was time to kick up her heels and see just what kind of man could fulfill her carnal desire. She got goose bumps just thinking about it.

Laurel took a deep breath. Okay. Right. That's it. Whoever she ended up with in this quiz—either the professional, the boy-next-door, the bad boy, or man-in-uniform, she'd seek him out and do with him what she wanted. Eventually, she would end up with a normal, sedate guy. But for now, she was young and free and she wanted to experience something crazy and out of control. Something her father would frown on. And there, the seeds of independence were sown, just a little root-grabbing hold for dear life.

She reached down to her purse and pulled out a pen, ripping the page from the magazine. Excitement tingled in her belly as she set the glossy page on top of the cover, and read the first question. Marking her answers, she moved through the questions quickly. She turned the page over to see who her hottie was and read the information.

Once more the door opened, and Laurel looked up expecting to see her father, but his PA was there once again.

"Don't tell me. He can't have lunch."

"He's very sorry, but the clients have insisted on taking him out to lunch."

Yes and the clients come first, she thought to herself as she set down the magazine next to her on the leather couch. Suddenly, tears stung her eyes, but she blinked them away. She didn't understand why he was acting like this. Stuffing the pen and the test haphazardly in her purse, she said to Lucy, "Thanks. I'd better get back to work."

"He really is sorry, Miss Malone."

Laurel grabbed up her copy of *SPICE,* her suit jacket and stopped at the doors. Smiling sweetly, she replied, "Sure. I know that."

She marched past the desks, her bag bumping her hip as she strode toward the glass doors and the exit.

THEODORE MACALLISTER TOLLIVER III wasn't easily impressed. But the woman who walked toward him dazzled him. Her soft brown gaze slid over him and away. He didn't seem to interest her at all. She was dressed conservatively, but the thigh-length form-fitting gray skirt showcased a stunning, eye-popping figure that appealed to him on every level. The V neckline of the woman's blouse dipped low, revealing her creamy throat, making his fingers ache to touch her smooth skin.

As she passed, something dropped out of her purse, but Mac was too preoccupied with the one question burning on his brain: "Who is that?" Mac whispered to his personal assistant Sherry Black.

Sherry looked over and narrowed her eyes. "*She's* the boss's daughter, Laurel Malone." She turned to face him. "You can forget it, buster."

"Why?"

"I've known her since we were kids. She doesn't date guys like you."

"Guys like me?"

"Yes, guys just like you. Men who work for her father are not even on her radar. She couldn't even describe what you look like because, buddy, you're invisible to her."

"Why doesn't she date guys who work for her father?"

"Because he would approve."

"And that's bad?"

"Yup."

"Because stockbrokers are boring?"

"With a capital *B*."

"Do you think I'm boring, Sherry?"

"You, Mr. Tolliver? No. You're a laugh a minute and so very charming."

"Angling for a raise, are you?"

"And so smart. No one could put one over on you."

Mac turned to go when he spied a piece of paper on the floor. He bent to pick it up and saw that it was a quiz from one of those women's magazines. *"Who's Your Hottie?"* he read and looked up at Laurel, now in a mouthwatering profile as she spoke to the receptionist at the front desk. He rose and was just about to walk over there. It would be a great way to meet her and get her to look at him. Really look at him. For some reason, he saw it as a dare. He wasn't invisible. He'd gone to all the right schools and done all the right things. He'd just gotten hired at Malone Financial Services exactly one week ago for double the salary of his last job. He had skills. She would see him if only she'd look.

But he stopped dead halfway there. In his hand was the blueprint of Laurel's idea of the perfect man. This piece of paper could give him an edge if he had the guts to fit her ideal mold. A sharp dose of adrenaline followed that thought. He could be the someone who made Laurel Malone do a double take. Somehow that made him feel a little bit better about her obvious lack of interest in him.

He looked down at the paper in his hand and back up at Laurel. Could he possibly give up this chance to see just how he measured up to what she desired in a man?

He reversed direction and went into his office instead, closing the door. He sat down behind his desk and studied the questions and how she'd marked them.

On the back were descriptions of four different types of men. They read:

6 or fewer points. The Professional.

This guy's goal-oriented, decisive and responsible. He goes after what he wants until he has achieved it and you can bet that means you. He'll use all his seductive, sophisticated powers until you surrender to him. This hottie is sure to light up your life with some red-hot romance.

7 to 14 points. The Boy-Next-Door.

Mom and apple pie are his watchwords. This fresh-faced, sensitive hottie will make you melt into a puddle at his all-American feet. Whether it's fixing your car or a leaky faucet, this hottie is always ready to help. But don't underestimate this guy's passion for you. It is red-hot, white and blue. This hottie knows how to set off fireworks every day of the year.

15 to 21. The Bad Boy.

The leader of the pack never follows the rules. He walks on the edge, calling his own shots and stirring up trouble. His devil-may-care charm will make your inhibitions dissipate for this hottie knows how to let loose and throw caution to the wind. He might be trouble, but oh what fun that could be. This hottie is a rebel who will get your motor running.

21 or more. Man in Uniform.

From the fire station to the police station to the U.S. military, there aren't many women who don't sigh over a man in uniform—all those muscles and courage. If you fantasize about being rescued, this is the man for you. This hottie who faces danger with such passion everyday can and will rock your world.

He added up her points and discovered that she had seventeen which meant that her hottie was a bad boy. Mac sighed. That kind of guy Mac couldn't understand. He wasn't cool or rebellious. He never stepped outside the barriers of what was good and proper. Why? Simple, he knew the value of hard work and of making his way in the world by playing by the rules. Breaking them was not in his makeup. He couldn't even steal a cookie from the cookie jar if his mother had told him no. He was much more in the professional mode, but he should have known that Laurel would want a guy as far away from the stockbroker type as she could get.

He wasn't in her league. Hell. He wasn't even in the ball park.

"So LET US GET this straight," Haley Malone said to Laurel. "You're going to have a hot fling with the next bad-boy biker you meet."

"That's right," Laurel said giving her sister-in-law a sideways glance. Thursday nights were reserved for her dinner with Haley, Dylan and Margo Grant. Margo was Haley's best friend and her husband's business partner. A year ago they'd opened SilverWire Partnership, an up-and-coming advertising firm. It was only after Haley's marriage to Dylan that Laurel became such good friends with the two women. The timing was perfect for her to talk to them both since she'd just made the decision that day to go after her bad-boy biker.

Laurel sliced into a plump plum tomato for the salad

she was in the process of making in Haley and Dylan's big kitchen located in Westchester County. After marriage, Dylan and Haley had moved out of the city, but they'd kept the Greenwich Village loft for the times they wanted to stay in town. Laurel approved of the big house they'd bought once they were married.

"And all because you did the *Who's Your Hottie?* quiz in *SPICE?*" Margo asked.

"Right," Laurel responded to the tall redhead currently sitting on the edge of the counter, drinking a glass of white wine.

Margo and Haley shared a look. "It doesn't seem like you would do something like that," Haley said.

"That's another reason why I'm doing it. All my life I've been the good girl. I want to change that."

Dylan Malone, Laurel's brother, came into the kitchen. "I see the klatch is busy at work. Mmm, it smells good though."

Haley smiled at her husband and opened the pot of chili so he could get a good sniff. "Now be a lovely husband and go to the store and get some French bread for me. You know the kind that I like."

"We need bread?"

"Yes, we do."

"Okay." He grabbed his car keys from the counter and minutes later they heard the door close.

Margo looked at Haley, and then opened the door that housed the bread. "Looks like French bread to me."

"We can't have Dylan milling about while we're talking about Laurel getting it on with a biker dude," Haley pointed out, rolling her eyes.

"True." Margo nodded.

"What if he mentioned it to Dad?" Haley added.

"He wouldn't do that," Laurel said, defending her brother.

"You know how guys are. Clueless," Haley said and then turned to Laurel. "So do you have any prospects?"

"Sherry Black from Dad's office is shopping for a motorcycle for her boyfriend, and her boss's brother owns a motorcycle dealership. So we're going there on Saturday."

"And you're going to shop for a guy?" Margo asked.

"Why not? It's a good place to meet men who ride motorcycles."

When both of her friends laughed, Laurel stiffened. "It's not funny. Do you have any better ideas?"

When her question was met with silence, Laurel narrowed her eyes. "See. It's not such a bad idea."

"No, it's not and you just gave *me* an idea," Haley said thoughtfully.

"What?" Laurel asked.

"If you find this guy and you do hook up with him, how about coming to a Who's Your Hottie party?"

"You just thought of this now?" Laurel asked, popping a small bite of tomato into her mouth. She shrugged. "Why not. I'm walking on the wild side anyway. He might as well know it."

"Great. We can put the invitation on *SPICE*'s Web site and the first fifty couples who RSVP get to come. How about two weeks from now, say on a Friday? What do you think?"

"Sounds like good publicity," Margo said, taking a sip of her wine. "And as for you Laurel, short of going to one of those scary biker bars, I guess it's not such a bad idea. You could meet some upscale bike-riding Romeo, I guess," she admitted.

"I don't care if he's upscale. He just has to be clean and groomed and have the attitude."

"What attitude?" Haley asked.

"That in-your-face attitude. Like he doesn't give a damn what anyone else thinks."

"You know those guys tend to be jerks," Margo warned.

"I won't tolerate a jerk and that's stereotypical. I'm going to keep an open mind."

Margo held up her glass. "To sex in any form, shape or manner," she toasted.

Haley laughed and raised her glass along with Laurel. "To sex," they all chimed.

"So LET ME GET this straight. You pick up a quiz that this babe in your office dropped," Mac's half brother, Tyler Hayes, said as he leaned against the wall of the repair shop. It was connected to the showroom by an open glass door, so that Tyler could keep track of customers browsing the brand-new bikes.

"That would be the boss's daughter."

"Good one. And she wants some bad-boy biker dude instead of a kind, sensitive guy like you."

"Bite me," Mac said, giving his brother a sidelong glance as he tried to loosen a bolt to remove the engine from the frame of the bike he was repairing. It was bright and early on Saturday morning and he was working with his brother in the motorcycle shop they owned together. Tyler did the buying and selling and Mac took care of the financial side, but he was a whiz with fixing motorcycles and enjoyed the work. To cut the monotony of high finance, Mac often enjoyed the physical labor of helping his brother whenever he had a chance.

"It's tough luck that when Mom remarried, you got the hoity-toity dad and the prep school name. And the prep school to go with it," Tyler commented. He knelt down to search through the tool box and came up with a wrench.

Mac accepted it and clamped it onto the bolt, but it still wouldn't budge. "Dad wanted what was best for me."

"Never said he didn't. Mom did good marrying Ted. My deadbeat dad doesn't even compare."

Their mother had married Theodore Tolliver II two years after Tyler's dad had left her. Mac was conceived almost immediately and was named after his father, but had always gone by the nickname of Mac to his family and friends. Mac was thankful he'd had the chance to grow up with Tyler. His other half brothers were much older and, therefore, didn't tolerate having a kid following them around. But, Tyler, only three years older, had taken his younger brother under his protective wing. Although Tyler was never interested in prep schools and college, he'd chosen entrepreneurship and starting his own business. He was closer to the rebel Laurel was looking for.

"So what is this chick's name?" Tyler nudged his brother out of the way and tried to loosen the bolt himself.

Mac nudged him back, grinning when the bolt refused to give even for his brother. "Laurel Malone."

The bell over the door rang and both Tyler and Mac looked toward the store's entrance. Mac recognized Sherry the instant she walked in the door. He retreated, not wanting her to see him. He prided himself on his professional reputation and didn't relish that the office would know that on weekends he turned into a grease monkey. He liked keeping his professional and personal lives separate. When he glanced at the door, things went from bad to worse. The woman right behind Sherry was Laurel.

"That's her," he blurted out, dropping the wrench on the floor with a metallic ring.

"What? The chick?"

"Yes. Laurel."

"What is she doing here?" Tyler asked.

"She's with Sherry. I told Sherry about you. She wants to buy her boyfriend a motorcycle. She and Laurel are friends. Sherry must have invited her along."

"Well, let's take care of that." Tyler started for the adjoining door, but stopped when Mac didn't follow. When Tyler turned, he gave Mac a quizzical look.

"I don't want them to see me. I have an image to uphold at work."

Tyler snorted. "Prima donna," he said snidely.

Mac calmly flipped him the bird, and then grinned.

"Get back to work, Cinderella," Tyler said, grinning back. "I'll handle it."

Tyler's teasing aside, he'd be mortified if anyone other than family saw him like this. He wasn't exactly dressed to kill. He wore his oldest jeans and they were a little too snug, a T-shirt that had seen better days— now the arms were ripped off—and his baseball cap was on backward to tuck in his hair. He didn't usually shave on Saturdays either because he knew he'd have to shower after working on motorcycles all day. Best to keep a low profile.

He pulled off the ball cap and tugged the bill over his eyes. Hunching his shoulders, he bent back over the bolt, doing his best to ignore the very sexy Laurel Malone.

LAUREL GAVE A quick look around the motorcycle dealership and was disappointed. There were men there, but most of them had a woman on their arm. The only guys who looked single was one man dressed in a business suit and who was clearly old enough to be her father, and the other two were eighteen-year-olds.

Her roaming eyes fell on a sweet little motorcycle tucked in the corner of the showroom. It was red and black with gleaming chrome. For some reason, it called to her and she walked over to it. She ran her hand down over the engine, the smooth metal cool to the touch, but heated something that had been dormant in her blood. She could see herself on this little baby, tooling down the highway, the wind in her face and the city to her back.

A little voice inside her piped up. *This isn't practical, Laurel. It's also dangerous and reckless.* The fantasy came crashing down. That little voice in her head was her mother talking, and it was stern and sensible. She couldn't seem to get past the disapproving tone. If she bought one, she'd have to deal with the voice *and* with her father's disapproval. Not a great combination. She could argue, but he'd put up such a fight, she wouldn't enjoy riding it anyway. Laurel was smart in choosing the battles she waged with her father; a motorcycle was low on the list.

Laurel turned her head and the salesman was standing next to her.

"Nice, huh?"

"Gorgeous."

"Hi." He extended his hand. "I'm Tyler."

"You're the owner. Sherry told me you're her boss's brother." He was attractive, maybe he'd be a good choice for her. He seemed like the kind of guy who would live on the edge.

"Sure am." He put his hand on the bike's seat. "This is a good selection for you. It's a new model, the Ducati Monster six-twenty."

"I love the name."

"And you'll love this bike. It's the lightest and easiest handling Ducati. The six-twenty offers a low seat height. Why don't you give it a try?"

She smiled and thought, *why not*. It's the closest she'd probably come to riding a motorcycle. She straddled the bike.

"Here's the new slipper clutch for seamless shifting," he said, indicating the feature with the toe of his black cowboy boot. "It's also got a new color matched front fairing, newly designed mirrors for increased visibility, and a comfortable, upright riding position."

"This is really nice, but…."

"The only caution I could offer is it's a powerful machine, but it can go from more aggressive sport to comfortable city driving, easy riding. It's got six gears to get your revs. It's responsive and fun. This is one maneuverable machine, a perfect choice for a slight body-type like yours. It's also easy to maintain. I can have it ready for you tomorrow."

"Let me think about it?" Laurel smiled and then her eyes fell on the guy working on an old Harley in the back. He was using all his strength to loosen something. His biceps bulged with thick muscle, his close-fitting, sexy jeans molded to his tight, fine-looking backside. A baseball cap covered most of his dark hair, but the thick strands at the back of his neck curled slightly. The ratty T-shirt he was wearing accentuated his wide, broad shoulders.

He had bad boy written all over him, and quite suddenly Laurel wanted him in the worst possible way.

Abruptly, he let go of the wrench and threw it on the workbench. Exasperation clear in every line of his gorgeous body. The movement caused the muscles in his arms and across his chest to shift temptingly as he moved. Her pulse quickened with female appreciation. He was so compelling, his magnetism so potent, she couldn't help but respond to his stunning good looks.

He reached down and grabbed a bottle of something and as he lifted it, he glanced up, his disarming gaze locking with hers—as bold, direct and unapologetically sexual as the man himself.

But then he broke eye contact and turned his back. Rude and unrepentant about it, he sure did have the attitude and it piqued her interest even more.

"That's my mechanic, but you shouldn't get any ideas about him."

Laurel felt as if she was coming out of a trance.

She'd forgotten that the salesman had been standing there and a faint blush heated her cheeks. "Why not?"

"He's not exactly the type of guy you want to bring home to daddy."

Perfect. Even better than she hoped for. "He's a rebel?"

"Sure is. He's got a wild streak and is too handsome for his own good. Been a chick magnet since he started producing testosterone. Unbelievably sharp, but he's got problems with impulse control. I'd fire him if he wasn't such a good mechanic and my brother, Mac Hayes."

"Another brother?"

"I've got three, counting...er...my half brother Theodore."

"That would be Sherry's boss, Mr. Tolliver."

He nodded just as Sherry came over and snagged the salesman's attention. Laurel couldn't move from the spot. Her bad boy had opened the bottle and was pouring some goop into his hand, then he swirled it around the piece he'd been trying to loosen.

He wiped his hands and, once again, grabbed up the wrench. His muscles bunched as he put all his weight and force into turning the bolt. It came free with a jerk, but he was off balance. His momentum drove his fist right into the metal parts of the engine. He yelped and shook his hand out. With a low expletive, he dropped the wrench.

Without thinking, Laurel moved through the open glass door into the repair shop. "Are you okay?"

The man looked up at her and stared. He stared so long that she shifted. "Let me see," she said as she reached for his hand. "You're bleeding. Do you have a first-aid kit?"

He inclined his head, causing a lock of sable hair to fall across his brow, accentuating his rugged appearance. "Over there on the wall," he said, still staring at her as if she was an alien being beamed down in front of his very eyes.

"But there's no need to make a fuss," he continued in that shivery low baritone, all the while attempting to pull his hand free.

"Are we going to get into an argument, Mac?"

The secret, wicked grin he bestowed on her made her lungs tight and sent her heart hammering into overdrive.

"Doesn't look like it."

From his shaggy hair and seductive blue eyes to his muscular, hard body, he radiated rough-edged sexual energy and drew her interest like no other man.

He looked like a big hunk of gorgeous trouble.

Acting bolder than she'd ever been in her life, she asked. "Where's the restroom?"

"Over there, but customers aren't allowed in here. It's too dangerous. You'd better get back to the showroom."

Was he trying to brush her off? she wondered as she followed his pointing finger to the first-aid kit. Laurel grabbed his wrist first. The kit was portable and she removed it from the wall before heading to the restroom.

Entering, she pulled him along with her and let go of his hand. It was a small area and with the presence of the sexy mechanic it seemed to shrink even more.

He wasn't going to get rid of her that easily.

2

You think your guy is sexiest when he's wearing:

a. a power suit and tie
b. a uniform
c. leather
d. denim

—*Excerpt from* Who's Your Hottie? *quiz,*
SPICE *magazine*

"WHY DON'T YOU SIT HERE," Laurel said, indicating the closed toilet seat. Mac sat. He raised his hand to his eyes.

"It doesn't look too bad," he said. "I can handle it."

"How can you tell through the grime?"

He flashed her a seductive grin. "Practice."

"Not the first time you've gotten a scrape, huh?" Beguiled, she smiled back. "You should wash so I can see the cut better." Laurel stepped away from the sink, but the tight space in the bathroom only pushed her closer to the mechanic.

"Hazard of the trade."

"I bet."

"I don't usually get a gorgeous Florence Nightingale to doctor me up though." He turned toward the sink and washed his hands with the soap nearby.

"It's Laurel Malone, not Florence Nightingale," she laughed as a flutter tumbled through her at his words. *Gorgeous.* He thought she was gorgeous. It wasn't a word she usually associated with her petite form, but the word on his lips made her feel ten feet tall. "I have to confess that I don't usually go around doctoring people," she said as she pulled some paper towels out of the dispenser.

"Judging by the no-nonsense command in your voice, I'd say you'd be good at it." His eyes watched her every move.

She shrugged. She'd never thought of herself as commanding. She wet the paper towels under the leaky faucet of the sink.

Almost every attempt she made to dab at the cut, he effectively ducked. "Mac," she said with exasperation. Finally she had to hold the back of his hand to keep him still.

With each movement, she tried to ignore how the shape of his head was beautifully curved, sleek, perfect, an irresistible temptation. His face filled her view, everything centering on its planes and hollows, its shadows and the intense blue eyes. *Where there's smoke...* She was suddenly caught up in that never-miss-a-thing gaze.

"How did you know my name is Mac?" he asked softly.

"Your brother told me," she responded breathlessly. "He tried to sell me that little Ducati you have in the window."

"Did you buy?"

"No."

"So then he tried to sell you me?"

"Not exactly. I noticed you first and wanted to meet you." Laurel spoke quietly, and her hands began to tremble.

His eyes were full of confusion and then twinkled with interest as he stared at her. When those sexy blue eyes shifted to her neck, her skin seemed to burn. With his right hand, he gently touched her throat. "Why?"

He sat so still, his breathing aligned with hers. His body filling the tiny room, his nearness wreathing her. When she shifted her gaze away from his, she caught her reflection in the mirror. She saw the soft pink in her cheeks, the way her lips were parted as if she were waiting for his kiss. Saw herself aroused.

She pulled her eyes away from her reflection, wishing she could splash some cold water on her face. She ignored his question, taking great pains to clean his hand. When she finished washing away the blood, she reached for the package of bandages in the first-aid kit. Her hands fumbled with the wrapping. Gently, he took the bandage and opened it for her. Just as gently, she applied it to the back of his hand. She leaned away from him, the small of her back pressed into the rim of the sink.

"All done," she said, her voice way too soft. She heard Sherry calling her name. She would get impatient if Laurel didn't answer. Impatient enough to come back here and catch her with this wildly interesting man. Suddenly, he stood up, his hip hitting her leg. He cupped her face. His eyes traveled over her. He caressed the skin of her cheek.

"I asked you a question," he said, his voice rough.

"You look exactly like the kind of guy I want to hang out with."

"What kind is that?"

"Dangerous."

"Dangerous," he said, his dark brows cocked.

All she could do was nod.

"So, I make your heart beat faster?"

"How do you know my heart is beating fast?"

He lowered his head and kissed the spot on her neck where her pulse beat rapidly.

The back of his hand trailed down her cheek to her throat and to the back of her neck. His thumb tilted her chin up. His mouth wavered over hers, and that sense of anticipation and aroused male enveloped her, surrounded her like a cape.

One of her legs was between his, and the press of his muscled thigh was unintentional, yet the pressure inflamed her. Dimly she pushed back her caution. This wasn't the time to worry about whether or not she could trust this guy. She was getting out of her comfort zone.

It was her chance to make her move—break out of her self-imposed prison.

He paused, as if he had his own doubts about kissing her. She acted. In that very moment, she was the one who brought her lips against his. She needed that kiss or she couldn't have taken another breath.

Beguiled by the scent, by the sudden heat flaring between them and the overwhelming temptation, she jumped into the unknown.

His mouth was soft and oh so tantalizing. She didn't think she could ever get enough.

The heat of his mouth seared every other kiss she'd ever received out of her thoughts and permanently out of her memory.

There was a wealth of passion in this man, and it reached out and engulfed her as easily as the unrelenting crush of a tidal wave against the shore.

He deepened the kiss, his sensuous lips flexing over hers in an urgent fierceness that left her breathless. She felt him spread those heavily muscled thighs to give him better balance, jerking her hips against him by sliding his big hands over her buttocks.

The pulsing heat from his groin reached out to her even through the heavy denim of his jeans and made her groan into his soft lips.

Mac pulled away from her, turning his head, cursing. She couldn't gather her thoughts.

"Laurel," he said his voice uneven, his breathing rapid, "your friend is calling you and she's right outside the door."

"Who?" The profile of his jaw was so strong and it was torturous being this close to his face. Why didn't he kiss her again?

He laughed shakily. "Your friend."

He turned back to her, and the heat in the bathroom seemed to go up ten degrees. "My friend…?" she said, getting lost in the crystalline blue of his eyes.

"The woman you came here with. She's probably finished buying a bike," he speculated, patiently explaining.

"Right, my friend. She's calling me," she said, trying desperately to focus.

"Now, Laurel." He stared at her and she felt her insides melting. "You have to let go of my neck," he said, amusement lighting his features.

She quickly realized that she still had her arms entwined around him. "Oh. Sorry," she apologized as he separated his body from hers and reasoning returned to her numb mind with a jolt. She could hear the footsteps outside the bathroom.

He moved away from her, and she felt bereft, alone. All she could think about was that toe-curling kiss. She brought her hand to her mouth, touching her tingling lips with the tips of her fingers.

"You go ahead. I'll wait until you're gone. She won't know we were in here together."

She knew she should go, but she felt rooted to the spot. She reached into her bag and pulled out a business card. Hastily she wrote down her home telephone number. "Call me," she said before she grabbed her bag and made her way past him.

MAC LOOKED DOWN at the piece of paper in his hand and couldn't believe that he had Laurel's number and that in the last five minutes she'd kissed him full on the mouth as if he was the most sexy guy in the world.

"Looks like you got yourself a number," Tyler said, standing in the bathroom doorway, his shoulder against the jamb and a self-satisfied smile on his face.

"What did you do?"

"Just a little misdirection."

"You told her I was a bad-boy biker?"

"Sure did."

Mac couldn't believe what he was hearing. "But that was deceitful."

"Excuse me, bro, you were the one eating your heart out over this woman. So she thinks you're not exactly who you are. Play it up. By the time she finds out who you really are, she'll be hooked."

"I don't know exactly how to be a bad boy."

"It's easy. Come on," Tyler said as he moved away from the door. Mac followed him out to the front of the dealership. Tyler walked directly to the clothing racks.

"Take these riding leathers."

"What are these for?"

"To protect your legs when you're riding, Einstein. It helps if you wear tight jeans underneath. Outlines the package."

Mac laughed.

"Don't laugh. If you think women don't check us out like we check them out, you're crazy. She was all goggle-eyed over your ass in those tight jeans."

"No way?"

"Way."

"Tight T-shirt in some silky material is good. Shows the pecs and biceps and the material is soft to the touch. Women like that." He handed Mac a slinky black T-shirt. "Also, the must have if you're going to show that you're a bad-boy biker—the leather jacket, preferably with lots of buckles and chains. Women think that's cool, too."

He threw the jacket over Mac's arm. Then he walked over to the footwear. "You'll need work boots in black, cowboy boots in black, and a pair of biker boots with lots of buckles again. Women are into the hardware."

Mac looked down at his groin and back up at his brother. "The hardware?"

Tyler grinned and said, "Yup." He slapped Mac on the shoulder and said, "Get yourself a few pairs of black jeans, black pants and some more T-shirts. White goes over good."

"You're suggesting that I use this quiz she took and seduce her like it's a strategic plan."

Tyler's forearm swung around his brother's neck into a playful headlock. "You're telling me you haven't thought of that? Why did you keep the test?"

Mac extradited himself and turned to look at his brother. He knew it was true, but the guilt inside him tightened. "It doesn't seem like a good way to start a relationship."

"Who cares? You're not supposed to be thinking like Theodore Macallister Tolliver the third. You're supposed to be thinking like Mac Hayes, rule breaker, heart breaker and all around tough guy."

"Right." Although she'd pulled him down to her succulent mouth, he deepened the kiss.

"Wouldn't hurt to get some tattoos."

"Tattoos? Someone repeatedly sticking a needle in me, no thanks."

"Chicks dig it."

"I'm not interested in chicks. I'm interested in Laurel."

"Look Mac, I'm just trying to help. I've never seen you so torn up about a woman. You have a lot to offer. I'd say screw her if she can't see you for who you are, but going after what you want takes guts and sacrifice. Question is: Do you want to tell her who you really are and run the risk of having no chance at all?"

The question lingered in the air between them. Mac's mind went back to that kiss, the anticipation of it. The feel of Laurel's hot, soft mouth, the way she molded her body to his was pure heaven. The texture of her creamy skin had been so silky beneath his fingertips. The full, lush promise of those firm breasts pressed against his chest. But more importantly, Mac couldn't forget the way she had looked at him right before she'd kissed him with everything she had. Those eyes held such life, such heart. They sparkled with fire and need. He couldn't ignore the way his whole being was clamoring for just another taste of her. There was something inherently special in this woman and he wanted her. "No. I don't want to risk that."

"Good. Now the bike. She's real interested in the Ducati Monster six-twenty."

"That's a tight bike. What color?"

"Red."

"Let's not be too conspicuous. I'll take the silver and black."

"Ducati it is. I have one that's just come in for a customer who cancelled. It's yours."

"You really think I need tattoos?"

"Look, I know this woman who does henna tattoos. They're not permanent, but last about three weeks. I don't think you'd want to or could keep up a deception longer than that."

"No needles?"

"No needles."

Mac followed his brother into the back of the dealership and stood by while he pulled the cover off the bike. He still felt that lying to Laurel was wrong, but he wouldn't lose his chance to be with her. After that intense kiss, he was sure there was something there. The masquerade would only be for a short time. He thought he could pull it off.

"This baby will get her juices flowing. A cool helmet and she won't be able to resist you, little bro."

"Let's hope so."

"One more thing. I told her you had a wild streak, impulse control problems and were a chick magnet."

Mac just stared at his brother.

"What?"

Mac took off his baseball cap and ran his hand through his hair. He closed his eyes. "Great. Just great."

BACK IN HIS LOFT, he was beginning to have second thoughts about the whole thing. Tyler's heart was in the right place; he knew his brother was only doing what he thought Mac wanted. The other side of the coin was that Mac wasn't so keen on trying to be someone he wasn't. He liked who he was, how he treated other people. He couldn't imagine being such a jerk. It went against the grain. He wasn't sure how good he was at pretending or if his own strong personality would still show through whatever act he tried to put on.

The biggest problem with his conscience was that this wasn't fair to Laurel. Sure, she'd get her fantasy man, because he'd try to be everything she wanted. Or thought she wanted. But reality always tended to be much different from fantasy and although he wasn't any prince, he certainly wasn't a knave, either.

After showering and getting a bite of lunch, he sat down at his computer and turned it on. Once the computer had booted, he dialed into the Internet and searched on the keywords "bad boy." After a moment of searching, the Web sites popped up.

Man-to-Man.com was one of the choices and Mac clicked on the link. It brought him to an article written by Ladies' Man. The article's title read, *How to Use the Techniques of a Bad Boy to Snag Women.*

He started reading. *Most men don't really understand what it means to be a "bad boy." They believe that bad implies treating women in a derogatory way. But a bad boy is basically a guy who doesn't bend to a woman's will or meets her expectations—this is what arouses her interest and earns a man the bad-boy label. In essence, being bad is good.*

The main difference between a typical guy and a bad boy? The bad boy places his needs before hers.

Just as he figured. Bad boys were selfish. He guessed he could take a bit of the author's advice. Mac really didn't have a clue about how to do this and he was in too far now to turn back. He printed out the article, poured himself a glass of juice and sat down to educate himself.

3

When it comes to sex, the moves that make you crazy are:

a. bold and adventuresome
b. suave and romantic
c. sweet and slow
d. hard and rough

                         —Excerpt from Who's Your Hottie? *quiz,*
                                        SPICE *magazine*

LAUREL WENT STRAIGHT HOME after she left Sherry at the dealership. She had enough time to indulge herself in her closely-guarded secret. It only took her moments to change into a white tank top and coveralls, along with a navy-blue sweatshirt to keep away the chill. After making herself a sandwich to eat on the way, she jumped into her SUV and drove out of the city.

Her whole body hummed and not only because she was getting away for a little guilty pleasure. It was Mac. The thought of those hot blue eyes, the way his mouth had moved over hers, the hard planes of his body which she wanted to explore. Her heart picked up its beat, making her feel like a teenager with a crush on the school bad boy. That was how he made her feel—young and vibrantly alive. And anxious to see him again. She hoped she didn't have to wait too long.

He looked like he knew his way around a bedroom and Laurel, although cautious about sex, wasn't a prude by any stretch of the imagination. It would be wonderful to throw off caution and have a purely physical and wild affair with a leather-clad biker. Imagining him decked out in leather and knee-high biker boots made her nipples tighten and her whole body clutch with excitement.

Forty minutes later she was in Cranberry—a quaint little town with a diner and a hardware store where checkers were played outside on warm, sunny days. She drove through the streets, feeling glad to be a part of this town, glad to get waves from the townspeople who knew her.

It was her secret life.

A life that no one, not even Haley and Margo or her friends and family knew about. This place was just for her.

She pulled up to a white clapboard house. It was small and run-down, but Laurel would get to that eventually. It was the detached garage, which she'd just finished renovating, that she headed for the moment she jumped out of her vehicle. She inserted her key into the padlock and opened the double-wide doors to let in the spring sunshine. The smell of wood, paint, and metal hit her the minute she turned toward the interior.

For some people, it was swimming, hitting the water, feeling their muscles contract and release, the quiet and the solitude. For others it was machines, racing around a track, adrenaline kick to the stomach, a punch of excitement and a roaring crowd.

For Laurel it was wood, the smell of it, the smooth grain against her hands, the satisfaction of a job completed, the moment when rough-hewn pieces became something she'd created.

Her modern shop had all the "toys" that she needed to do her creating, a shop that even the most advanced craftsmen would covet. She had built an L-shaped workbench with cabinets and a board to hold all her necessary tools. Tools that had been accumulated with as much pleasure as searching for that perfect dress or those perfect heels. She had measuring tools, hammers, screwdrivers, saws, drills, clamps, tools to sand with and safety equipment to protect herself with.

She smiled as she stepped inside and the leftover sawdust scraped along her work boots. She should have swept that up, but she'd been in too much of a hurry the last time. She'd had dinner plans with her family in the city and she didn't want to be late and have to explain to them why. She hated lies.

Secrets were something else. They had to be protected at all costs. It wouldn't do for her father to find out that she'd bought this house in Cranberry. That she'd spent a good portion of the trust her mother had set up for her. Using the money Mom had left her gave her great satisfaction. Her mother had wanted her to do something special with it. She had been adamant before she died that Laurel must find a good use for it. *Don't leave it to multiply and multiply. After all, you can't take it with you.* She'd taken those words to heart.

Her father wouldn't find anything worthwhile about her passion for eclectic furniture or carpentry. Inside her workshop, she walked around and checked to make sure that all was in order. She inspected the half-done frame for the chair that would eventually look just like a pair of lips. She had yet to buy the red fabric, but it would make a nice addition to her bedroom.

She pulled off her sweatshirt, already heated by the glorious sunshine streaming in through the four skylights she'd installed on the roof. Ready to get down to business, her attention was drawn outside when she heard the scraping of metal cans and an uttered oath.

She left her workshop and spied Mr. Hayes picking up his metal can from the curb. She walked over to him. "Mr. Hayes, how's it going?"

Jeffrey Hayes was her next-door neighbor. He was retired and enjoyed living the quiet life in Cranberry. Mr. Hayes liked to grow things and can them. He sold his produce at the farmers' market and his canned peaches were to die for.

"Just fine, Miss Malone. And you?"

"Good."

"I can see that. It's always good when you get a chance to get something done in your workshop, brings a sparkle to your eyes." He stared at her for a moment. "Hmmm, seems there's a bit more color on your face today. What could have put that there, I wonder?"

She smiled wider, knowing that it was Mac. Odd. Mac Hayes. Mr. Hayes. "I've sort of met a guy."

"Oh, I see. That'll do it."

"Yes, he's an exciting guy," she added, reaching down and picking up the cover to the garbage can.

"One of those fast city boys."

"He rides a motorcycle, wears leather."

"Make sure you wear a helmet."

"I will," she promised and followed him up his driveway. Mr. Hayes continued, climbing up the creaky stairs to his house.

"Speaking of danger, those stairs look like they're in need of repair. I'll fix 'em for you," Laurel offered.

"But, you have furniture you want to build. There's no need, I'll call a carpenter."

Laurel gasped. "Mr. Hayes, don't you dare. Let me do it...and all I'll expect in return is an invitation to one of your wonderful lasagna dinners. My mouth's already watering."

"Sounds like I'm getting the better part of the bargain." He gave her a sly look. "I'll make you a deal. You finish your project first, and then you can do my stairs."

Laurel thought for a moment as if it was a weighty decision. When Mr. Hayes gave her a goofy look, she smiled and laughed. She reached out her hand and shook his. "Deal."

She practically skipped into the garage. There was a lot to look forward to. The lip chair, the chance to go to the lumber yard to purchase more wood, and Mac. Exciting, glorious, gorgeous blue-eyed Mac. Her whole body just tingled thinking about their next encounter.

HE WAS STILL saying "great" to himself as he walked into the henna shop Tyler referred him to. Mac had gone home first, showered and shaved, sort of. He'd left a little bit of stubble on his face. He figured he needed all the help he could get. The other thing he'd done was to let his hair go free form. It was a mane of hair that he tempered with product and a comb, but left to its own devices it was a crazy shaggy, curly monster. In the shop there was a heady mix of eucalyptus and henna and other exotic scents he couldn't pinpoint. He walked up to the woman standing behind the cash register.

Mac was wearing the biker leathers over tight jeans, the boots, a white T-shirt and the jacket. It had surprised him that when he'd gone to the store to buy the tight shirt, the female sales clerk had tucked her number just behind the buckle of the belted leathers. She'd given him a flirtatious smile, too.

Flabbergasted, he'd gone to his bike at the curb and had to dodge two gorgeous women checking out his bike, then him. Now this woman's eyes were glazing over. Geez, didn't any of them see him?

Why was he complaining? It was what he wanted Laurel to do when she saw him.

The woman at the cash register addressed him before he could speak. "Hi there. What can I do for you?"

"My brother sent me. Tyler Hayes."

"Right. He said you wanted a couple of tattoos. Do you know what you want?"

"No, uh, not really."

"Why don't you come over here and pick out something?"

He went around to the back and looked through the designs. What would a wild, impulse control, chick magnet pick?

"How about this crouching panther?"

"Where do you want it on your body?" She looked pointedly at his butt. Mac blushed. He was sure a chick magnet *did not* blush. He turned away. "Uh, back of my left shoulder."

"Okay."

He could hear the disappointment in her voice. Was his butt that good? Sexy even?

He was so pathetic.

"What else?"

"This barbed wire around my left bicep." He endured two hours of having the tattoo artist use every trick in the book to get his interest. But he only had interest in one woman. Laurel. He was doing all this crap for her and her alone.

Once he was free to go and had paid for the tattoos, he tried to decide his next move. He should call Laurel and ask her to go out with him.

Scratch that.

He should do something impulsive. He needed to ride over to her place. Problem. He didn't know where she lived. Wait. He was being extremely dumb today. Maybe it was the spell Laurel had cast over him. Duh. He could look her up with his pocket PC. That task accomplished, he jumped on the gleaming Ducati and roared away from the curb. When he reached her brownstone, he brought the bike to a stop.

He let his breath out slowly. He was so damned nervous. He was usually calm, cool and under control. When he'd interviewed at Malone Financial Services, he'd negotiated his salary with all the aplomb of a man who had ice water in his veins.

He went up to knock on her door, but an SUV pulled up just as he raised his hand.

Laurel got out and his heart stopped in his chest. She was so beautiful in the waning light. Her dark hair shone, pulled up in a haphazard ponytail. She hadn't noticed him yet, but went around to the back of the SUV and opened the hatch.

She was intent on something in the back. He walked down the stairs and came up to her.

"Laurel."

She jerked and her head hit the top of the vehicle. Smooth, jerk wad, he thought to himself as she focused wide, excited eyes on him.

"Hey, babe." He wrapped his arm around her waist and brought her close and tight against his body. His mouth clamped onto hers before she could say a word in greeting or protest.

She clasped her hands around his biceps for balance. A murmur broke against his lips.

He continued the kiss, sliding his arm to the small of her back, sending his hand over her beautiful ass. It hadn't been his intent to kiss her. The impulse sneaked up on him, but it was perfect. Inspired.

The scent of her rose up around him. It was clean and spicy and sweet. Intensely female. An unexpected twist that no article could prepare him for. He inhaled her essence like a man who'd been trapped underwater and had finally reached air.

Her scent mingled with her taste, just as silky sweet, and a wealth of unbelievable sensations, the yielding tenderness of her lips, the satiny wisps of hair at the nape of her neck, her baby-smooth skin. She swamped his senses.

She shuddered in his arms like a leaf caught in a gentle breeze. Everything faded away but the real weight of her against him and the frantic desire to entice her to go deeper with him in a soul-searing kiss.

When they parted, they were both panting for breath. He looked down into her wide dark eyes.

She licked her lips. "Mac? What, what are you..."

His mouth ached to feel hers again and he changed the angle of the kiss going for devastating and dazzling. He pulled her body flush against his, cupping the hot skin at the back of her neck. She gasped against his mouth. When he finally let her go, he was trembling more than she.

She inhaled raggedly as he stepped back and sent her a wicked, sinful gin. "Outstanding, babe." He cupped her cheek and smoothed his thumb over the softness. "I'm glad you gave me your number."

"Me, too. I don't think any man has ever blown me away like that."

"I do what pleases me and you please me," he stated matter-of-factly. It was his mantra.

"I do?" she asked on a sigh, looking up into his face. He couldn't get enough of staring into those eyes.

"Absolutely." He turned his attention to the back of her SUV. "What were you trying to get..." his words trailed off as he saw the bright end of a chair. "Damn," he said softly as he pulled the piece toward him. "A chair shaped like lips. This is amazing."

Laurel put her hand on his arm, her warmth touching him through the leather.

"You like it?"

"It's original. Where did you get it?"

"A...small town outside of New York."

"It's really different." There was also a side table with an inlaid top of many-colored wooden pieces. "I'd like to know where. There's a perfect place for it at my...er, friend's." He caught himself just in time. He had a sophisticated, upscale loft that screamed professional, not wild streak, impulsive, chick magnet. But he could see this chair sitting in his living room making a statement. The table, too. "Maybe someday you can take me out there. This table is inspired."

"So why are you here?" she asked as he pulled the chair out of the back of the SUV. Laurel grabbed the table and they carried the pieces toward her brownstone.

"You're coming with me...for dinner," he said in a commanding voice. Sounded impulsive enough.

"It's pretty short notice."

"Spontaneity is my middle name."

She stuck the key in the lock and turned to look at him and laughed. "Right. Who needs uptight and serious? We need fun. Where are you taking me?"

"I don't know yet. I'll surprise you." He hefted the chair through the door. "Where do you want this?"

"You can set it right there against that wall. I'll take it upstairs later."

He set it down.

"I just need to shower."

"I brought something for you to wear."

She turned to him, her face alight. "You did. Let me see."

"I'll go get it."

He went to his bike and picked up the package, the contents of which he'd spent a lot of time picking out for her.

He brought it into the house and handed it to her.

She took it and beamed at him. "Make yourself at home. I won't be long."

She raced upstairs. Mac checked his appearance in

the hall mirror before walking into her living room. It was an elegant room with elaborate, white crown molding. The furniture looked handcrafted and shone with a luster of being highly polished and lovingly cared for. The hardwood floor was covered by a thick throw rug in rust, green and gold. Above a rust-colored couch was a stunning oil painting of the Green Mountains in the fall. The trees a beautiful accent to the colors in the room.

It looked like Vermont. He'd been skiing there at Smugglers' Notch and Killington. Both resorts were spectacular.

He heard the shower go on upstairs and he tried not to think about Laurel naked.

True to her word she took only twenty minutes. When he heard her coming down the stairs, he stood in anticipation.

She entered the room. The black leather pants that he'd bought her fit perfectly. But his eyes were drawn to her breasts, beautifully displayed and creamy against red lace revealed by the open white cotton blouse tightly buttoned just under her cleavage. He'd scoped out the store until he'd found someone that looked to be her build and asked her her size. The woman had taken one look at him and volunteered to try on the pants. Afterwards, she asked him out. He explained he was buying a gift for his girlfriend. She'd told him if he ever dropped his girlfriend to give her a call.

"You look...great."

She'd pulled her hair into a tight ponytail on top of her head. She was stunning.

"Thanks. I forgot to tell you how sexy you look. You look wonderful in leather, just as I imagined."

His brother had been right. She'd checked him out, thoroughly.

Mac shifted, not used to all this female attention. He said, "Is that a painting of Vermont?"

"Yes, I bought it there last year. Have you been?"

"We've been there skiing."

"You ski?"

"Sure. Why?"

"You don't look the type."

Damn, already he'd slipped up and he'd only been with her for a few minutes. Then he remembered his half-brother Tyler barreling down the mountain on a snowboard. His brother insisted that chicks dig it because it was so daredevil. "Actually, I used a snowboard," he bluffed, walking toward her.

"A snowboard? That takes some skill." She preceded him into the foyer, opened a closet door and grabbed a cropped red leather jacket to wear.

He breathed a sigh of relief at having restored his image. He grabbed her hand and led her out of the house. At the bike, she stopped.

"Wow, this is way cool. Way, way cool."

He handed her a helmet and she put it on. He put on his and straddled the bike. She climbed on behind him and he gunned the engine just for effect before he moved away from the curb.

The Ducati handled like a dream. He'd ridden heavier bikes and was pleased to find this one easy to maneuver with a rider on the back.

When he came across the Wolf Pack Road House,

he made a quick turn and parked the bike with the other motorcycles clogging the lot. Rowdy music blared out of the bar.

When they walked toward the place, Laurel touched his arm. "This looks kinda rough."

"It's okay. No problem," he said trying to act like he thought a bad boy would. No fear of dark and scary places, no fear of taking a sweet, beautiful woman into one of them. He could protect her.

Once inside he realized that he was totally out of his element. It was so crowded that they pressed up against people as they moved toward the bar. He spied small round pub tables and booths in a couple of rooms, but they were full of talking, laughing people. When he reached the bar, he brought to mind the article. *Walk the talk* it imparted as advice. *The difference between a bad boy and a nice guy is that when a nice guy goes to a bar, he'll let the lady order first and then say, I'll have the same. A bad boy knows how to be a gentleman and also lets the lady order first, but when it's his turn he orders something strong and takes it in one gulp. That'll impress a woman every time.* "What would you like?" he yelled at Laurel over the blare of the music.

"A beer is fine," she yelled back.

The bartender came up to them and he ordered Laurel's beer and then said, "Bourbon, straight up."

The longer he was in this place the more uncomfortable he felt. The bartender set the beer and the glass of bourbon on the bar. Mac picked up the glass and threw back the contents in one gulp. The liquid burned all the way down. He coughed and Laurel placed her hand on his shoulder.

"Are you all right?"

"Went down the wrong hole," he wheezed back. Smooth, he thought to himself.

To keep up appearances, he pretended to enjoy the strong taste of the alcohol as it brought tears to his eyes, pretended to enjoy the blaring music that made it impossible to talk, and pretended he was having the time of his life.

He ordered food for them from the menu and indicated to the bartender that they would go sit.

He hated this place and he hated the way some of the men were looking at Laurel. In her red leather jacket, she stood out like a beacon. "Why don't we find a table," he hollered over the music and she nodded.

They made their way to the back, and Mac snagged a table as a couple left. He helped Laurel off with her jacket, trying to be nonchalant about all the stares directed her way.

Thankfully, the music ended and the band announced they were taking a break. The noise level in the roadhouse evened out.

She reached out and snagged the hand he'd injured in the bike shop. "How're the knuckles?"

"Okay. It was just a scrape."

She turned his hand over. Looking down at his palm, she traced the base of his fingers and frowned. "Do you like being a mechanic?"

Mac didn't really know what he should say. He enjoyed working on the bikes, but it was the manipulation of money and the stock market that he loved best. He felt he should stick as close to the truth as possible. "I enjoy it."

Her eyes went to his. "What is it about fixing bikes that you like?"

"What do you mean?"

"Skill. Specifically skill with one's hands. I was wondering if that's what you like about it. Using your hands."

He was getting distracted by the way she was running her fingertips over his skin. "I like to use my hands, Laurel," he replied. He could imagine how it would feel to move his hands over her body, over those luscious breasts.

She met his eyes, and he saw she hadn't missed his meaning.

"You have very few calluses. Do you use a pumice stone?"

A pumice stone? What the hell was a pumice stone? "Ah, yeah. Works like a charm."

He cupped her hand in his and ran his thumb over her palm noticing slight nicks and calluses along her fingers."

"What is it that you do, Laurel?"

"I'm a senior analyst, a fancy name for an accountant. Maybe you've heard of the firm? Waterford Scott? One of the big five."

Waterford Scott was one of the firm's clients. He remembered seeing a statement for them. "No." He lied. He didn't expect that a man like Mac would know anything about the corporate world at all. "So, how does a woman who works at a desk all day get cuts on her palms?"

Her reaction was instantaneous. She withdrew a hand and wrapped it around the bottle of beer, then took a sip. She shook her head sharply. "No way. I don't know you well enough to divulge my secrets."

"Sounds personal," he said gently, trying to ease her anxiety in talking about something that was important to her.

"It is." Her lips pursed in agitation, and her demeanor was defensive enough that he fully expected her to tell him to go to hell, that it was none of his business what secrets she harbored, but beyond her tough act there was a hint of vulnerability in her gaze. It squeezed his heart.

His attention was immediately piqued. He'd thought he had Laurel pegged. Hmmm. The hardworking good girl had facets. The unexpected discovery was like finding a diamond in the rough. The waitress came and dropped off their meals.

Wanting to forge a connection with Laurel, he smiled, reaching out his hand. "I'm not going to make you share."

She didn't hesitate to respond to him, and the trusting gesture gave him an odd jolt of guilt. This ruse didn't entitle him to her trust, but he wanted it anyway.

As he began to take Laurel's hand again, meaty fingers reached out and closed over her wrist.

Shocked, they both looked up to see a burly, denim-clad man with a goatee standing there staring at Laurel.

"Let's dance," he growled as the band started up again.

When Laurel looked at the intruder, the cretin spoke again. "Don't let this joker stop you. Come on."

And with that, he shifted his hand onto Laurel's arm

and brought her up. Mac stood. Laurel tried to free her hand from the man's grasp, but he wouldn't let go.

It happened so fast that Mac didn't have a minute to respond. He'd opened his mouth to protest, to tell the guy to back off, the burly guy shifted and coldcocked Mac right in the face. The blow rocked him back on his heels and he grabbed the table for support. Mac felt the warm trickle of blood from his nose and the metallic taste of it oozed from a cut cheek.

The man laughed and sputtered, "Who are you trying to be, Midnight Rider? Ha!"

The cretin tightened his hands around Laurel and the situation looked like it was drastically getting out of Mac's control. There were so many people in the bar that the bouncers up front didn't even know that he'd been punched.

Quickly regaining his balance, his face throbbing from the blow, Mac hauled off and let one solid left hook fly, knocking the guy into a table of patrons.

The guy came up off the floor and lunged at Mac, but this time Mac was ready. His fist connected squarely with the guy's jaw and he slumped forward.

Mac shoved him off and two bouncers dragged the man away. "You wanna-be bikers make me sick," he shouted at Mac.

People hooted and hollered. Though Mac was only interested in Laurel, as he gathered her into his arms.

4

You have a hot date tonight. What would you choose for underwear?

a. that little black thong,
b. plain Jane white
c. bikini sexy
d. wow 'em boy briefs
        —Excerpt from Who's Your Hottie? *quiz,*
                      SPICE *magazine*

THE BRACING CHILL of the wind made her press her face tightly to his back as they rode through the night. The scary incident at the Wolf Pack Road House was behind them, but the adrenaline still buzzed through her system. He'd been magnificent in his protection of her. She'd never had a man fight for her in her life and there was something primal and savage about it that hit her at her core.

It excited her beyond everything.

She'd lived such a sheltered life and for the first time she'd gotten a little taste of what it really offered. Her whole body tingled; her senses heightened, her nerve endings sizzling with energy.

She pushed her pelvis against his backside because

she needed the relief the touch brought. She felt his body jerk slightly and willed them to get to her brown-stone faster.

When he pulled up outside, she grabbed his arm and dragged him toward her house. He pulled against her hold and she turned to him.

"What?"

"Are you sure you're up for me to come in? I don't want to intrude on your privacy."

She looked at him as if he'd grown horns. She didn't want this polite man asking her if she was all right. "It's not tenderness, nor privacy that I want right now, Mac."

"What is it you do want?"

"You."

He swallowed, another weird thing that didn't seem to mesh with the man, the leather and the bike, but she was beyond deciphering him, beyond waiting.

"Come on."

He followed her up the stairs, waited while she opened the door.

He tried to stop her again. "Are you sure about this Laurel? Really sure?"

She leaned forward and grabbed ahold of the belt of his leathers and jerked him inside. She slammed the door and without preamble pushed him against it. Her mouth found his. She was hungry for his strength, his heat. Breathless with anticipation. Maddened.

This was what she had been missing, passion for life. Heat, sweat, energy. She felt it all pulsating through her. That little voice tried to talk her out of taking this man right in the hallway of her conservative brownstone, but she pushed that voice aside and silenced it.

The sense of power sped through her, beating in time to her racing heart. She wrestled with his jacket as her mouth devoured his. Something heavy hit the floor just before the leather, but she paid it no heed, more interested in getting his T-shirt off. When he protested, she pushed him harder against the door, holding his wrists tight in her grasp.

He whispered softly when she removed her mouth, "You want to be a bad girl, Laurel?"

Vibrating with lust and need, she slid her hands over his glorious chest, the muscles hard and thick beneath her hands.

"Slow down, babe. Slow down."

"I don't want to slow down. I want you, Mac, now." Now that the time had come to take that first step into unfamiliar territory, she wanted to know if he would be game for anything uninhibited and unadulterated. She wanted to be assured that he was what she was looking for.

She wanted a man dominant enough to take her beyond and be open enough to let her do the same with him. She wanted aggressive sex, not gentle, polite or altogether civilized. She was sick to death of civilized.

His brows raised in surprise and a primal light flamed in his deep blue eyes.

"Surprised?" she asked.

"Yes. I thought you'd be the missionary type. Not so it seems."

"No."

"You want to show me how bad you can be?"

She shivered with a blend of panic and excitement.

"I don't want to show. I want to take."

He was so close to her she could feel the heat of his body through his clothes, could inhale how deliciously male he smelled—a heady combination of heat and forbidden passion. His warm breath ruffled the wisps of hair along the side of her face, and pure, undisguised sexual energy crackled between them. It was a rare and irresistible chemistry that intensified with each moment that passed.

Her body softened, melted, undeniably readying for his possession. No words were spoken as she lifted a hand and curled her fingers around the nape of his neck. She pulled his lips to hers and kissed him deeply, ardently. His mouth was just as hot and willing, his tongue daring and ravenous, consuming her with rich, pure pleasure.

They pulled back, just long enough for him to quickly strip off his T-shirt and yank off her jacket and shirt. Their mouths met again, lips open, teeth nipping and nibbling, tongues touching, tangling. Her hands swept over the broad expanse of his chest, and she plied his nipples with her thumbs, then brushed her fingers down to his taut belly. With a groan, he smoothed his palms along her shoulders and pushed her bra straps down and her bra off, so that it dropped to her waist. He didn't waste any time in cupping her breasts in his hot hands, rolling her nipples back and forth between his fingertips.

She felt out of control. Yet she luxuriated in the untamed sensation, along with the freedom to do things with and to this man that she'd never explored with another lover before. Like indulging in mindless, uninhibited sex for the pure, captivating desire of it.

But ultimately, Mac was a man she instinctually trusted with her body and more. A man who made her feel amazingly feminine and lavishly seductive—as if she were made specifically for him, in every way. And for as long as their affair lasted, she *was* his, in every way.

Breathing hard and aching for that fast, frenzied joining, she blindly reached for his belt buckle and released him of the leathers. As they fell away, she unfastened the top button and pulled the zipper of his jeans down over his hard, erection. Grabbing the waistband of his jeans and briefs, she shoved both down to his thighs. His iron-hard shaft sprang free, and she encircled him with her fingers and stroked his length, using her thumb to smear the bead of pre-come that had gathered on the head of his penis.

His entire body jerked in response. He slanted his mouth across hers again with a tough growl, his tongue thrusting deep as he reached down to get her out of her leather pants and underwear. When the fabric dropped to her ankles, she kicked it out of the way.

Hot, callused hands skimmed up her thighs, and long, seeking fingers delved into the crease between her legs. She was already wet, already unbearably aroused, drunk on passion and the excitement of the forbidden. He found her clit with his thumb and stroked across that knot of nerves in a sleek caress. All it took was that one electrifying touch, and she came in a fast, powerful climax that left her panting and gasping for breath.

She wrenched her mouth from his and pushed him back onto the bench in her hallway. She bent down and grabbed her purse, pulling out a condom no single girl was without. He sat down and she sheathed him. She moved toward him, spreading her legs wide open on either side of his thighs. Bracing her hands on his shoulders, she sat astride his lap, and his cock slid along her slick flesh and unerringly found the entrance to her body.

She pushed her hips down at the same time he bucked upward, sinking onto his hard heat, closing around him to the hilt. She inhaled sharply at the exquisite sensation of being wholly filled by him, and he groaned, long and low. She rocked her pelvis against his, his body tense and quivering. She grabbed onto his shoulders again, easily picking up the rhythm he set, and rode him with utter abandon.

His hand roamed up her spine, and his fingers fluttered along the nape of her neck, then wrapped the strands of her hair in his fist. He tugged her head back with that one hand and used the other to splay against the middle of her back, forcing her body to arch into him and her breasts to rub against his chest.

Their bodies were locked tight, and she continued to ride him as he scattered soft, damp, biting kisses along her throat and over the upper slopes of her straining breasts. He circled his tongue around one rigid nipple, blew a hot stream of breath across the peak, then did the same to the other. He lapped at her slowly, licked the taut tips teasingly, and nibbled until the madness was too much to bear. Grabbing a handful of hair from the back of his head, she pressed his parted lips to one aching, tingling crest in silent demand, and he obeyed, taking as much of her breast as he could inside the wet, velvety warmth of his mouth.

He sucked and she felt that pulling sensation all the way down to her sex. She couldn't stop the whimper of need that slipped from her lips, couldn't hold back the convulsions that started deep inside where Mac filled her, full and throbbing. She moved harder, faster, and came undone as a torrent of sensation gripped her limbs and sent her careening into an intense and fiery orgasm.

He released a harsh groan of surrender then and rocked her in time to each frantic upward surge of his thick shaft within her. She wrapped her arms around him, holding him close as his own body shuddered in and around hers in long, deep, powerful spasms.

When it was over, they clung to each other, their arms and legs entwined, both of them too wiped out to move. Chest to chest, the wild beating of their hearts was all Laurel could feel, and in that seemingly endless stretch of time, the profound connection between them was all that mattered to her.

MAC RUMMAGED through Laurel's refrigerator for a late-night snack. They'd been too busy getting out of the Wolf Pack Road House to worry about eating. Laurel had gone upstairs to take a quick shower and change into something more comfortable. He'd promised he'd stick around until she returned, and the truth of the matter was that he didn't want to leave, even though his bad-boy persona was expected to do exactly that.

Oh damn, he was in trouble here.

In fact, Mac was drowning. He knew this was a bad idea. Sleeping with Laurel tonight wasn't what he'd planned to do. Changing from mild-mannered Theodore to wild thing Mac gave Mac much more than he bargained for. The female attention, the instant respect, and the exhilarating fight all cumulated into a heady buzz. Why fight what he wanted? He'd donned this whole persona to give her something that she wanted, and to his surprise, found a resonating chord inside him.

He grabbed up a bowl of pasta and put it in the microwave, zapping it for two minutes. Searching through her drawers, he found a fork. As soon as the beeper went off, he dug in.

It didn't surprise him that he liked being with Laurel and that it was no hardship at all. She was intelligent, brave, and a lover he was sure he wouldn't be able to get enough of. The three facets were intrinsically joined in a way that fulfilled an emptiness within him he hadn't even known existed until she'd come along and filled that solitude with her exuberant presence, her fortitude, and even her moments of vulnerability.

He leaned against the counter and looked down while he ate. Strewn across the counter were clippings and photographs of a woman. One particular clipping caught his attention. The caption read: *Anne Wilkes Malone hands Melanie Graham, Curator of the Metropolitan Museum of Art twenty million dollars to create a wing for the preservation of art deco artists.*

Another clipping caught his eye. "*Anne Wilkes Malone, a native New Yorker, was born May 22, 1954, and passed away on June 17. Mrs. Malone is survived by her husband, William Tarlton Malone, her daughter Laurel Anne Malone and her son Dylan William Malone. Mrs. Malone graduated from Nightengale-*

Bamford and attended Vassar College in Poughkeepsie, New York.

Mrs. Malone assembled the world-renowned Anne Malone Collection of Art Deco art, which became a permanent part of the Metropolitan Museum of Art, punctuated by the large compilation of Jacques-Emile Ruhlmann....

"I see you helped yourself to my Alfredo."

Laurel's husky voice drew him from the article, and he turned his head as she walked barefoot into the kitchen, a soft smile on her lips. She was dressed in a pink muscle T-shirt with *Debutante* scrolled across the front and a pair of gray silk drawstring pants. Her hair was damp and in one long ponytail down her back. Her face was washed clean, and her skin pink from her shower. He caught the scent of freshly washed hair, and his stomach clenched. He ached to bury his face in her neck, to lose himself in the softness of her fragrant skin. He wanted to take her upstairs and pull her down with him and drift off to sleep wrapped in her arms.

Oh, yeah, he was definitely in trouble here.

"Guilty. It's damn good."

"I also see you're rummaging through my personal stuff."

"I couldn't help it. You're mother was Anne Malone?"

"You knew my mother?"

"No." It seemed every time he turned around he was putting his foot in his mouth. He couldn't tell her that his mother was on the Met's board and he'd met Laurel's mother once at a big social function. "I know of her."

"Oh, you follow women philanthropists?"

How was he going to extricate himself his this? She looked so skeptical and it was warranted. Why would a bad-boy mechanic have any knowledge of Laurel's mother? Pressing his hip against the counter, he crossed his arms over his chest and opted for the truth. "I remember reading about her when she donated her considerable collection of art deco paintings and furniture to the Met. That's all. Why do you have all these clippings out?"

The suspicion in Laurel's eyes dissipated. "My brother, his wife, and I are putting together a celebration of my mother's life. We have decided to have an auction for up-and-coming artists to honor her. We're trying to figure out where to host it. Those clippings are going to be arranged in a scrapbook and set in the wing for people to look through."

"You're father isn't involved?" The words escaped his lips before he thought about what he was saying.

She turned away without replying, bracing her hands on the counter, she looked down at the photos and clippings, and blew out a long stream of breath. She lifted her gaze to his, the depths of her eyes brimming with a wealth of emotion. "He's been very busy and doesn't really have the time to plan. He's leaving it up to us."

There was so much more she wasn't saying.

Walking over to her gleaming cappuccino machine, she prepared to use it. Her back was to him, her stance tense, making him think that she deliberately hid her expression from him, so that he wouldn't be able to scrutinize it. What she didn't realize, however, was that her tone, rough with strain, gave her away.

"Sounds to me like it's a sensitive subject," he said casually.

"It is." She pressed down on the handle to sieve the coffee from the grounds, and turned to face him again. "My dad is very particular about his work. He's increased the time he's spent in the office over the year since my mother's death. It's become his focus."

She spun back around and reached for two cups. "Do you want one? It's decaf."

"Yes, thanks." His gaze snagged on the bare skin of her waist, tantalizing him with the smoothness that he ached to caress with his fingers, taste with his tongue.

He refocused on the discussion, pushing those sensual thoughts from his mind. "Why do you think that is?"

She glanced at him, her expression closed and shuttered. He barely knew her and it didn't surprise him that she was reluctant to talk about something so personal, but he wondered if she had an outlet at all. She bit her lip, and lifted her chin, giving him a direct look. But beneath the shell of bravado was a hint of shyness that drew him like a magnet. Looking deeper into her eyes, he could also see a desperation that made his gut tighten.

A long sigh escaped her soft mouth. "I don't know. We don't communicate as well as we did when my mother was alive. Do you think we could talk about something else?"

She effectively ended the conversation with those words and Mac nodded.

Did she intend to keep him at arm's length because he was just her temporary bad-boy lover? "Sure," he said shrugging as if he the frustration in him wasn't tangible. The more he was around this woman, the more he wanted to know about her.

She finished making their drinks, the steamer making a racket as she heated the milk. She leaned forward and handed him the hot cup of cappuccino.

"So now that we have had sex and you know intimate details about my life, it's my turn to ask some questions."

This could be good or bad depending on what she would ask him. He liked the idea that she wanted to get to know him—it showed that she was interested in him. He wanted time to breach her barriers, and divulging intimate details was a good place to start.

"Shoot."

"You have a brother who owns a motorcycle dealership and one who's a stockbroker. Why a mechanic?"

"It's fun and the hours are flexible. I like to come and go as I please."

"A loner, huh?" she asked, moving past him. She headed into the living room, sat on the couch, curled her feet underneath her, sipping her coffee gingerly.

He followed her into the room and sat down next to her on the sofa. "Nah, not really. I like people, especially you," he said leaning close with a mock leer.

She laughed and pushed at his shoulder. "I didn't thank you for the leather pants. That was really thoughtful of you to buy them for me. Do you usually do that on first dates?"

"Not usually, but you seemed so caught up with the motorcycle thing, I wanted to give you a small part of that fantasy."

She set the cup down on a coaster on the small end table. Cupping his face, she smiled, dazzling him.

"It was wonderful. You gave me everything I could have hoped for. It's been a while for me. Dating and men haven't been a priority for me since I've been trying to make partner at Waterford Scott."

"I'm sure that corporate-ladder climbing is important, but, Laurel, a beautiful, desirable woman like you shouldn't bog yourself down with work. Is that why you came looking for me?" He didn't know how he wanted her to answer, he knew why she came looking for him, but he hoped she was seeing less of the bad boy and more of Mac.

"Partly. I've been pretty good all my life and I wanted to see how the other half lived. Promise me something." She looked at him from under her lashes, mischief shining in her eyes.

"What?" he asked warily.

"That you won't laugh."

He grinned then. "Why would I do that?"

She nudged him. "I'm going to tell you something embarrassing."

He wiped the grin off his face. "Okay. I won't laugh."

"The real reason I went looking for you was that I took this quiz in *SPICE* magazine."

"What quiz?" he asked nonchalantly, his stomach tightening.

"Who's Your Hottie?"

"I'm your hottie?"

"Yes—"

He started to laugh and Laurel put her hand over his mouth, laughing herself.

"You promised you wouldn't."

He kissed her palm and she laughed harder.

"Now, I want to ask you something important, so get serious," she said, trying to keep a straight face.

"Okay."

"My brother's wife is the editor of *SPICE* and she wants me to attend a party the magazine is going to throw. Interested in being my hottie escort?"

This was probably a really bad idea, but her adorable, pleading eyes made him forget everything but doing as she asked. "Do I have to wear a tux?"

"No. That's the beauty of it. You can wear what you normally wear. They want to showcase the *Who's Your Hottie?* quiz for publicity. Do you mind?"

"No. I'll go with you."

"Now you tell me one thing that you'd be embarrassed if someone knew."

He smiled. "You've got to promise never to tell."

"I promise."

"I rent Kung Fu B-movies and go over to my grandmother's house and we watch them together."

She covered her mouth and laughed. "You do not."

"Do. She loves them."

"You love them, too," she accused.

He stared at her a moment, then a slow smile creased his cheeks. "I do," he admitted just to see her smile again. "Does it tarnish my bad-boy image?"

"Maybe just a little." Do you want to go upstairs?"

"I'd better get going," he said and winced inside. He really wanted to go back to bed with her, but he knew what was required of his new persona.

"All right."

She got up from the couch. He followed her to the entryway, his eyes drawn to the sexy way she moved her hips as she walked, breathing in the heady fragrance of a desirable, willing woman.

In the hall, he picked up his T-shirt and pulled it over his head. She was already holding his leather jacket. He took it from her and slipped it on. She watched him keenly, with sensual brown eyes that seemed to consume him.

She took a step, brushing against him to open the door, but before she could complete the move, he lost the battle with himself and he pulled her up against him, his mouth finding her lips soft and inviting.

Laurel sighed, her body molding to him as she sank against his chest, her groin resting against the plackard of his jeans. She pressed hard against his mouth, using body language to tell him that she didn't want him to go.

An involuntary groan escaped him. He wanted nothing more than to strip her out of her sexy clothes, press her against the wall and take what she was so eagerly offered. Every nerve ending in his body was on fire, pulsing to the beat of his heart.

Through the haze he remembered why he was doing this. It was a long-term plan. If he didn't let her go now, he was never going to be able to. His raging hormones would take over and he'd break an important rule.

Rules were made to be broken, he thought, but not this one. He had to handle everything correctly.

He pulled his mouth away from her tempting lips, and saw the anticipation in her sexy eyes, an ardent need. He took a much needed step away from her.

"I'm outa here," he said, his tone gruff.

She licked her lower lip, and, gracefully accepting his decision, opened the door for him. "See you."

Her eyes captured him, dark deep pools that riveted him to the spot, and he lingered, unable to leave her gaze. "So long," he said, and hightailed it before he changed his mind.

5

It's hardest for you to resist:

a. dessert
b. gossip
c. shopping
d. sex

—*Excerpt from* Who's Your Hottie? *quiz,*
SPICE *magazine*

"NICE SHINER. What the hell happened to you?"
Green eyes, almost identical to his own blue, scrutinized him.

"Give me a beer," Mac demanded, pushing his way
past Tyler. After leaving Laurel, Mac had gone to his
brother's apartment in lower Manhattan. Tyler could afford a pricey loft like Mac, but preferred not to.

"Mac..."

"Now, Tyler."

They made their way to the kitchen. Mac sat down
at the table and ran a hand through his hair. His brother
grabbed a cold one out of the fridge and set it down in
front of him before he swung a chair around and sat.

"So what happened?" Tyler took a sip of his own
brew and leaned back preparing to wait patiently.

Mac grabbed the bottle and took a gulp. "I took her to a biker bar and got into a fight."

Tyler's mouth quirked in amusement. "I'd hate to see the other guy."

"Yeah. He looks worse for wear."

"Sounds like you enjoyed yourself."

"I did. It was exciting. I've never experienced that before. Although I have no idea how I'm going to explain this black eye." He shot his brother an amused look.

"Okay, so did the chick get pissed and drop you?"

Mac shifted in his seat, a bundle of pent-up restless energy. "No. On the contrary, it turned her on."

"You're kidding me. You already..."

"She's damned amazing." Mac wasn't going to give any kind of detailed report. He wasn't the kind of man to kiss and tell, no matter what role he was playing for Laurel's benefit.

"So what are you doing here?"

"I'm acting like a no-commitment bad boy, just like she expects me to."

"You left her?"

He kept staring straight ahead and nodded.

"Did you want to leave?"

"Hell, no. I hate games." With a painful twang of his heart, he knew he wanted to see this woman again, but he couldn't let her know it. I don't want to hurt Laurel, but I'm supposed to skip out after making love with her, right?"

Tyler sighed. "You're right. It's the kind of thing a bad boy would do. But it's not really the kind of thing you would do."

"I feel like a total jerk." Especially about making love to her. It was dangerous to get so intimate the first time you were with a woman.

"I say go with your gut on this. It hasn't failed you yet."

"I should go home. Thanks for the beer."

"No problem. Hey, we can have lunch later if you want."

"Right, and it's on you, Sensei, for getting me into this mess in the first place."

"McDonald's it is, grasshopper."

"Cheapskate," Mac muttered with a smile.

As he made his way down the stairs, Mac knew it was no use. He couldn't keep away from her.

THE SOUND OF a car alarm woke her. She rolled over, her eyes flickered open at the noise. She lay still for a moment, groggily assessing her surroundings.

Pushing her tousled hair back, Laurel paused for a moment as her fingers caught in a knot. She worked it free. When she disentangled herself from the bed sheet, her eyes came fully open.

She came completely awake, but her memory was still full of Mac and last night. She went to the closet and took out a colorful Japanese-style robe and slipped it on, tying it quickly.

Walking over to the window, she released a breath, leaning weakly against the window jamb. Mac. The emotions churned like a whirlpool within her, each one receding to be replaced with the next. Embarrassment, shock, and sweet slivers of delight accompanied each mental fragment. She'd acted completely out of character. Her senses had been altered, and wasn't it glori-

ous? Her eyes slid shut, seeing again that flash of
hunger on his face, so sharp and keen it had pierced her,
as well. For that one second, just for an instant, she'd
caught sight of a flash of guilt mingled with a pleasure
so intense it had taken her breath away.

She had no regrets about initiating and participating
so fully in such decadence. Maybe there was something
more compelling than the sight of a man, looking like
he'd die for the chance to touch her, but she couldn't
imagine it. It had been enthralling, tempting and so
sexy that even the memory had the power to send fresh
shivers through her.

Her eyes opened and her head tipped back. She
could be dishonest with herself and pretend that it was
just a one-night stand, but for her it hadn't felt that illusive. It had happened because she'd wanted it to. And
Mac was more, so much more. Could their affair really
progress to something permanent?

Touching him had been an incredible high. Running
her hands over that broad torso, freely examining the
jut of his erection as she wanted to.

There hadn't been any romantic props and none were
required. Just need, edgy and fierce, which had passed
from her to Mac and back again. She'd never before experienced a joining so urgent that it turned to roughness,
from a man visibly fighting his control.

Although she could feel her face wash hotly at the
recollection, she'd enjoyed tempting Mac to give up
that control, and had reveled with him in its loss.

Her arms slipped around her waist and hugged tight.
If she tried hard enough, she could almost feel the assured clasp of Mac's arms.

She didn't hold his leaving against him. She knew what she was getting herself into when she'd hooked up with a bad boy, so she had no one to blame but herself.

Why had he left? she wondered.

A splinter of unease stabbed through her. It was Sunday, so neither of them had to work, unless, of course, he'd had to go to the bike shop. That was a possibility. But the longer she thought about it, the more troubled she grew.

What if he hadn't left because he had to, but because he wanted to?

Maybe last night hadn't meant anything at all. She took a deep breath. Well, either way, she would weather it the best she could. Besides, she told herself sternly, she couldn't fall for him. He was a coming of age, a rebellion, a stopgap until she found the right guy.

Mac's brother had been right. He wasn't the kind of man she could bring home to her father.

She turned away from the window and walked back to her closet.

She would go to Cranberry and start a new project. It would keep her mind off Mac. It was no hardship to return to her favorite place. Just then, she heard the phone ring. Her heart leapt in her chest. Mac!

But when she picked up the receiver Haley's cheery voice came over the line.

"Hi, Laurel. I was wondering if you wouldn't mind if I borrowed your Kenneth Cole for the Met tomorrow. I don't have time to shop."

"No problem. Just let yourself in. I'm about to go out."

"Thanks."

"Oh, uh, by the way, my hottie and I will be attending the *SPICE* party, just let me know the particulars."

"Great. I ran it by my staff and they're all for it. My Web mistress will put the invitation on the Web site on Monday. You, me and Dylan are still meeting for lunch on Monday to discuss your mom's memorial, right?"

"Yes. If my plans change, I'll call. Bye."

Laurel replaced the receiver, disappointed that it hadn't been Mac. She dressed in a frayed work shirt and overalls with tears at the knees. Grabbing up her purse, she went down to the foyer. Just as she was about to open the door, she spied a shiny object near her planter. Bending down, she scooped up the item. It was a hand-held PC and Laurel frowned. Who could this belong to?

Then her confusion cleared. It had to be Mac's. Strange device for a mechanic to carry, but you didn't have to have a nerdy job to be a computer geek, she thought. She dropped the device in her purse and went out the door.

MAC AND TYLER WERE just finishing up lunch, when Tyler said, "Do you have your schedule for next week? I'd really like your help at the rally."

Mac put his hand in his jacket pocket looking for his handheld PC, but came up empty.

"Damn," he muttered.

"What's wrong?"

"I think...I dropped it at Laurel's. If she opens it—"

"She'll know."

"I'd better get over there now."

Uncertain whether going back was the bad-boy thing

to do or not, he figured he had no choice. He wasn't quite ready for the truth to come out.

He arrived at Laurel's in record time. Knocking, Mac fidgeted, unable to wait until she opened the door.

It would be a disaster if she found out about him now. He wanted the opportunity to know her better, especially after last night. He had every intention of telling her when the time was right.

This wasn't it.

When the door opened, it wasn't Laurel who stood there. A very beautiful blond woman, clutching a black-lace dress looked at him quizzically, then her face cleared.

"You're looking for Laurel, I'll bet. Sorry to disappoint you. I'm her sister-in-law, Haley."

"She's not here?"

"No. She had to go out."

"Do you know where?"

"Sorry. She didn't say, but we do find it odd that she disappears on the weekends without telling anyone where she's going, even her friends. I could try her on her cell."

"Would you, please?"

Laurel had a secret, Mac thought, as he waited for Haley to complete the call. He wondered what it could be. What could that innocent, unassuming girl be doing behind her family's back? It added another layer to an already fascinating person.

"I'm sorry," Haley said, "she's not answering."

With any luck, the darn thing was still here. "Look, I left something here last night. Could I come in and look around for it?"

"I don't know. Laurel's not home."

"I promise that I'll be quick, if you don't mind waiting. It is important."

"Well, okay, but if you could hurry, I have more errands to run."

Mac stepped over the threshold. He wasn't exactly sure where the PC would be, but it had to be somewhere nearby.

He scanned the floor and looked under the bench Laurel had there, but he couldn't find it. "Damn."

"No luck?"

"No. Do you know when she'll be back?"

"Oh, no. You've got to go." Haley grabbed his arm and steered him to the door.

"Why?"

"That's Laurel's father in the driveway and I don't think you'll want to explain anything to him."

The coffee he'd drunk at lunch went sour in his gut. Crap. He was in for it now. "You got that right," he said to Haley. "Nice to meet you."

He slipped on his sunglasses and made his way quickly out the door and down the stairs. Just as he reached his bike, he could hear Mr. Malone ask who he was. Haley's answer was lost in the revving of his engine. He sped away from the curb feeling as if he'd just dodged a bullet.

LAUREL STRETCHED the electric-blue fabric, with tiny silver circles, over the frame she'd built for the sofa. She'd painted the wood silver and the contrast of the fabric and paint gave her exactly the effect she'd hoped for.

Busy almost all day with her project, so much so, she'd ignored all her calls. She welcomed the diversion of carpentry, paint and fabric. Shutting out the rest of the world was why she'd come to Cranberry in the first place. But she couldn't seem to escape her thoughts. She'd spent too much time thinking after Mac had left her brownstone—thinking about the incredible hot sex they'd shared and how good it had felt to let go in a way she'd never done before. She'd held nothing back, mainly because Mac had been so receptive to her demanding moves. She'd been bold and dominant; he'd been generous with his body. She smiled secretly to herself, thinking about how greedy and utterly shameless she'd been. Not that Mac seemed to mind at all.

Despite how tired she'd been after their time together, she'd tossed and turned for a while, as her mind replayed the conversation with Mac about her mother—an intimate conversation, one she'd never intended to have with him. Odd that it would seem as if he knew her mother. And his explanation about seeing her donation in the newspaper just didn't ring true.

But her relationship with Mac was short-term and purely physical and, out of self-preservation, shouldn't have crossed over into anything emotional or personal.

Yes, he'd been persistent, but she could have refused to talk if she'd really wanted to. Instead, she'd allowed herself to be swayed by his questions, willingly so with that deep, mesmerizing voice of his, his soothing touch, and the genuine interest she'd seen in his eyes. It had been so easy to open up to him, to reveal details of her and her mother that should have remained private. It had been so long since a man had made her the sole focus of his attention and treated her as if he really cared about what she had to say, and she'd taken advantage of Mac's listening ear. After giving away so much about herself, she was now doubly curious about him, especially, as she glanced at her purse on the workbench, about the handheld PC she'd found in her foyer this morning.

Despite sharing part of her personal history with Mac, there were a few emotional issues she'd managed to keep to herself. What she hadn't revealed was the crushing sense of regret she'd lived with, since her mother's death, having drifted away from her dad. The fact that he had neither showed interest in, nor agreed to participate in the memorial for her mother hurt and caused a rift she wasn't sure how to mend. She couldn't understand his lack of support. Laurel knew that her father truly loved her mother, so it was particularly disturbing that he didn't find it imperative that something special be done for her on the anniversary of her death. The problem was that Laurel hadn't pressed him on the subject. In fact her ability to rise to the occasion and be confrontational in a situation was tempered by her upbringing.

Her mother had taught her to be a lady and ladies never were forceful or aggressive. So, she'd been unable to ask her father straight out why he was acting as if he didn't care.

At least with Mac, she knew where they stood with each other right up front. He wouldn't be sweeping her off her feet, yet she instinctively knew he wasn't a man to take advantage of anyone. Least of all her. Not when she was participating fully in her very own coming-out party. One she certainly wouldn't be wearing a white dress to—like she had to her debutante ball. She giggled, thinking decadent thoughts about Mac taking her in her white virginal dress. She wondered if it would even fit. She laughed again at the silly thought.

Using the staple gun, she attached the last of the fabric. Wiping the sweat from her forehead, she walked over to the workbench. She eyed her purse while she picked up and unscrewed the cap of her water bottle and took a swig.

It would be a breach of his privacy to open it and take a look. Wouldn't it? She warred with that little voice in her head and the voice won. She'd hate to have her privacy violated by someone she was even starting to trust. She looked down at her watch and was alarmed at the amount of time she'd been in her garage. It was going on six-thirty.

Pulling her cell out of her purse, she flipped it open and saw that Haley had called four times. She debated on whether or not to call her, then decided that Haley's house was on her way. She could stop in briefly before heading home.

It took her a half an hour to clean up her area and a few more minutes to secure her house and workspace. Traffic was light on the road and she was soon pulling up to Haley's place.

Dylan was just setting the trash at the curb and he waved at her as she slipped out of her SUV.

"Doing your manly duties, I see," Laurel teased.

He smiled and slipped his arm around her shoulders, giving her a quick hug. "Hey, to what do we owe this visit?"

"Haley called me and I was out, so I thought I'd drop by on my way home."

"Great. We were just about to have a late supper. Do you want to join us?"

"That sounds good. It'll give us a chance to talk about the auction details and I'm famished."

When she and Dylan entered the house, Haley screamed, "Laurel, where have you been? I've been trying to reach you all day."

Dylan gave his wife a quizzical look and Laurel wondered what had happened to put such a frantic look on her face.

"Dylan, could you get the chicken out of the oven and dish up the potatoes for me," Haley asked sweetly, with a very telling nudge toward the kitchen. She smiled brightly. Too brightly.

"All right. I'm going and leave you two to your girl talk."

Haley grabbed Laurel's arm and pulled her into Dylan's home office. Awards hung on the walls over a contemporary teak and walnut workspace. There was an impressive brick fireplace with trendy knickknacks and an oriental rug covered the hardwood floor.

Haley flipped on the light and shut the door, dragging Laurel to the camel sofa with the round back that she'd made for them for Christmas, but had to pretend she bought it.

"What's up and why all this subterfuge? I don't think Dylan was fooled." Laurel said wryly.

"Your biker friend was at your house today and Dad saw him."

Laurel gasped. "Oh no, what did he say?"

"Your biker friend?"

Laurel rolled her eyes in exasperation. "No, Dad." Although, Laurel wasn't sure what her father's reaction would be. In his present state, maybe he wouldn't care who Laurel dated. Somehow that thought upset her more.

"He asked me who your biker friend was and he didn't look happy."

"What did you say?"

Haley's eyes were contrite and her voice wavered. "I fell down on the job, Laurel. I'm sorry. I blurted out the truth."

Laurel's jaw dropped and there was a rushing in her head. "Oh my god! You told my dad about the quiz and that I trawled a cycle dealership for a bad-boy biker?"

"No," Haley said looking affronted. "Do you think I'm that simple? I told your dad you were dating him."

"Oh damn."

"I know. I should have come up with something better like he was looking for directions."

"Haley, don't panic. I'll smooth it over. What did he want?"

"Your dad?"

Laurel shook her head in frustration. "No, the biker."

"Oh, he said he was looking for something."

"Right, his handheld PC."

"He has a handheld PC?" Haley asked, then paused frowning. "That's weird. Did you look in it?"

"No!" Laurel jumped off the sofa and began to pace.

"I have no problem doing it. Let me have it."

She stopped pacing abruptly. "Haley!"

Haley gave her a sidelong look. "Come on, you're dying to look."

"Haley, Laurel, if you're done with your girl talk, dinner's getting cold."

"We have to eat," Laurel said, effectively ending the discussion about the PC.

Haley followed Laurel out of the office. "By the way, that guy was sizzling hot."

"Haley. You're married, to my brother no less."

"Yeah, yeah, yeah," Haley whispered as they approached the kitchen. "My husband is very sexy and I love him desperately, blah, blah, blah, but I'm not dead, you know. Your biker has the most beautiful eyes and that mouth. Yowza. No wonder you…"

"You're going to be dead if you don't get off this subject."

"So you did do the dirty deed," Haley said knowingly. "And who could blame you."

Laurel stopped so abruptly that Haley bumped into her. Laurel turned and gave her The Silent Death Stare. "I'm not going there. At least not now and not on an empty stomach."

Haley totally ignored her. "Okay, spoilsport, but Margo and I are going to want details later."

"Margo knows all about this?"

"Of course, she's my best friend and I had to have someone to dish to since you were quite unavailable. Where were you, anyway?"

"Wow, that chicken smells great," Laurel said.

The chicken tasted great, too, and since it was getting so late, she let Dylan talk her into spending the night. Laurel could easily borrow some things from Haley, since they were almost the same size.

Lying in her brother's guest room bed, Laurel wondered how her father would react to Mac. Maybe they could finally have a conversation that included more than the weather or how she was doing at work.

Now that she was reminded about her job, her thoughts went unerringly to what tomorrow would hold. Would Mr. Herman take away the Spegelman account and undermine her authority with the analysts she oversaw, or would he leave it be?

Nervous knots tightened in her stomach at the thought of conflict. She just wasn't good at confrontations, not a skill she'd picked up or was encouraged to learn.

She reached out to turn off the light, deciding that a good night's sleep was what she needed. She was exhausted. Her hand hit her purse and it fell, dumping the contents onto the rug. Laurel swore under her breath and she got out of bed to pick up the items. When her hand curled around the PC, her curiosity got the better of her.

She got back onto the bed and set the device on the nightstand. During dinner, she realized that she couldn't call Mac and let him know that she had his property—she didn't have his telephone number and when she asked Haley if she'd gotten it, she said she didn't have a chance to before Laurel's father showed up.

Lying down, she turned off the light, but the illumination from the bedside clock reflected on the PC's cover. She was sorely tempted.

MONDAY MORNING DAWNED and Mac still hadn't been able to get ahold of Laurel. He'd called her yesterday all day until it was late. Where could she be?

He wasn't able to stop thinking about the fact that Laurel could open the PC at any time and discover his true identity.

His gut twisted. What they had shared the night before was beyond his expectations and he quite simply wanted more. More of her body, more of her time, more of her.

He knew he would have to tell her eventually. He imagined what he'd say to her, how he'd explain who he truly was, the surprise and shocked expression that he hoped wouldn't shift to anger and recrimination.

Maybe she'd already opened it and discovered who he was and was avoiding his calls.

After lunch, his assistant popped her head into his office. "Mr. Tolliver, Mr. Malone would like to see you."

Mac looked up at Sherry standing in the doorway. His heart beat hard in his chest. Had Mr. Malone recognized him after all? Okay, he was just jumping to conclusions because of his guilty conscience. Mr. Malone probably wanted to see him about a business matter.

"Mr. Tolliver?"

"Yes, I'm going," he said and got up from his desk. He rounded it and passed Sherry who looked worried. Was that because she knew something was wrong, or was she worried about his lapse?

"You look tired, Mr. Tolliver. That's quite a black eye. Are you okay?"

Mac nodded. "I'm fine. Walked into a door," he mumbled. "Couldn't get to sleep last night, either." He buried his hands deep in his pockets as he walked toward Mr. Malone's office. When he started out this charade, it had been a challenge to make himself over to look like what Laurel wanted, to get her interest, to get her to pay attention to him. Now, after spending time together, he realized what he would lose if she found out about him, too soon. The complication of her father recognizing him as the biker who had been at Laurel's house yesterday would put a kink in his seduction plans. He wanted Laurel to be so taken with him, she'd overlook his little deception, but if her father got involved, it could mean exposure and likely, his job.

He walked up to Lucy, who was seated at her desk. "Mr. Malone is expecting me."

Lucy picked up the phone and buzzed her boss. After a brief conversation, she said, "You may go in."

Mac walked toward the heavy oak doors. It was surprising how different he felt from a week ago. Confident, focused, and determined. Today, he was a basket case, not sure what he would say to Laurel's father if he knew it had been him at Laurel's house.

He opened one of the doors and stepped inside. Mr. Malone was at his desk waiting.

Mr. Malone's eyes raked over Mac as he approached him. *Damn. He knows. He recognizes me from yesterday.*

Suddenly, Mr. Malone got to his feet and extended his hand. Mac was taken aback. He'd expected demands for an explanation, an apology, not to be welcomed.

He spied a picture of Laurel on Mr. Malone's credenza. She was smiling up at the camera, her eyes sparkling. He knew now he wanted to find out everything he could about her.

"Tolliver, good to see you. Have a seat."

Mac sat down. "Same here, sir."

"I knew I'd made a good decision in hiring you." Mr. Malone leaned back in his chair and eyed him with a wily smile on his face.

Mac shifted. He wouldn't think that if he'd realized that he was Laurel's "biker." He'd be mad as hell. "Why's that, Mr. Malone?"

"Call me Bill." He leaned forward in the chair, eagerness lighting up his face. "I've just received a call from Kevin Coyle at Coyle and Hamilton."

"He was one of my clients at Lockhart-Titan."

"One of your biggest, correct?"

"The biggest."

"He wants you to handle his portfolio and has left Lockhart-Titan for Malone Financial Services."

Mac felt weak with relief. "I'm glad he was that pleased with me. I'll continue handling his account with the same professionalism, Mr....ah...Bill."

"Good. He's expecting you downtown for a meeting in an hour."

Mac started to rise.

"There's another matter I'd like to discuss with you and it's of a delicate nature."

"Yes, sir." Mac sat down again.

"It's about my daughter."

"Your daughter?" Mac's mind went into overload and started churning up explanations to answer him.

"I want you to meet her."

His stomach dropped and he jerked forward in his chair. "No."

Mr. Malone looked at Mac sharply.

"Is there some problem with my daughter?"

"No. I meant it's going to be hard in the next couple

of weeks. My schedule is full." Oh hell, this was just what he needed. "Why do you want her to meet me?"

"It seems that she's gotten herself involved with someone completely unsuitable."

"And?"

"Well, you come from a good family. You're a man on the fast track. *You're* supremely more suitable. When would be a good time?"

"Could I let you know?"

"Surely, but don't make it too long. I don't want Laurel to fancy herself in love with this...biker. Also, let's keep this conversation between the two of us."

Mac held it together until he got to Sherry's desk. She wasn't there and he leaned down, bracing himself against the edge. Talk about a tangled web. Mr. Malone was worried about him, in his bad-boy disguise, pursuing his daughter. The phone started to ring. He should laugh it was so damn funny. He ran his hands through his hair and picked up the receiver. Absently, he said "Tolliver."

"Mac?" Laurel Malone's voice sounded in his ear. He closed his eyes.

What a tangled web indeed.

"Is IT YOU?" Laurel asked, shocked that Mac would answer Sherry's phone.

"Yes. It's me. Hey, babe."

"What are you doing in…" Her confusion cleared. "Oh right, you're Mr. Tolliver's brother. Are you visiting him?"

"Yes...um, no. I'm dropping off the invoice for your friend."

"Sherry?"

"For the bike she bought on Saturday."

"Oh. I was trying to reach Sherry."

"She's not here."

"Well, the truth is, I was trying to get ahold of you."

"Great. Tell me where, when and what you want to hold."

She laughed. "How about tonight and you surprise me like you did before. I really like your kind of surprises."

"Okay. See you."

"Mac, wait. I need…." It was too late. He had hung up. Laurel placed the receiver in the cradle and sighed. She'd originally called Sherry to find out if she'd ask her boss for Mac's number. She wanted to return his property, mostly so that she wouldn't be tempted to open it. But in truth, she wanted to see Mac again.

All day yesterday she couldn't stop thinking about him. She'd almost opened the PC a couple of times, but always at the last minute, she couldn't do it. Even though she knew she shouldn't, she wanted Mac to trust her.

It was a moot point, anyway. She couldn't imagine their affair lasting for very long. However, she was going to explore this man inch by delectable inch in every physical way possible.

Her thoughts were interrupted by a knock on her door. "Laurel? Are you going to the staff meeting?"

Laurel's stomach immediately tingled with butterflies and she reached for her notebook with clammy palms. She would hear about the Spegalman account and then she would have her say. Force herself to reply in a rational and calm manner. She could do it. She hadn't toiled here only to have her hard work go for nothing.

"Sorry, I'm coming right away." Laurel clutched her notebook and walked purposefully to the conference room. Mr. Herman and her subordinates, including Mark Dalton were all seated. Mark glared at her as she made her way to the conference table and sat down in the only vacant seat.

"Thanks for joining us, Ms. Malone," Mr. Herman said, his voice full of reproach.

Laurel cringed inside but charged ahead with a detailed update of her staff's progress on various projects. As soon as she was finished, Mr. Herman started talking about new business and congratulated two of her subordinates for bringing in new clientele.

His attention turned to her. "There is one more order of business before we adjourn," he said, his eyes unwavering. "Laurel, since you have quite a few demanding accounts and need time to acclaimate, I'm going to pull the Spegelman account and give it to Mark."

Say something, her brain screamed at her, the butterflies in her stomach fluttering frantically. She felt frozen and all her arguments seemed to fly right out of her head. She opened her mouth to speak, but nothing came out. All eyes turned toward her and Laurel wanted to crawl into a hole. "Thank you, Mr. Herman," she said lamely.

Her answer ended the meeting. She looked at Mark again and saw the self-satisfied smile on his face.

She sat there paralyzed until everyone left the conference room. Everyone but Mark.

"What's the matter, Laurel, nepotism got your tongue?"

Stung and disappointed at her inability to stand up for herself with Mr. Herman, Mark's comment caught her completely by surprise.

"What do you mean?" she asked

He snickered and gathered his papers. "You know what I mean."

"No, I don't," she said, getting up from her chair on shaky legs.

"Sure. I believe that," he replied and left the room.

Okay, that was interesting. What could Mark have meant by his comment? As far as she knew, Mr. Herman never showed her any favoritism, nor had he particularly praised her for her work. Come to think of it. That was strange. She'd accomplished quite a bit here and had excelled in her job. No one could say that she hadn't. So why all of a sudden did she feel as if she'd gotten something she didn't deserve. She could handle the Spegelman account and she could pull in new business. She'd done it before. Maybe that's what she needed to do—bring in a big client to prove to Mr. Herman that she was capable of doing this job. She might not be able to verbalize the reasons that she deserved the Spegelman account, but she could very well show Mr. Herman and Mark Dalton what she was made of.

Walking slowly down the hall to her office, she was brought up short by her breathless assistant.

"Kelly, what is it?"

"There's a man waiting for you in your office."

"I don't have any appointments." She frowned. "Do I?"

"No. Believe me. This isn't a client."

"Who is it?"

"He's wearing black leather with one of the finest backsides I've ever seen."

Laurel looked toward her office. Through the open door, she could see a nice view of Mac's backside, definitely fine and definitely encased in tight black leather. He moved around her desk and sat in her chair, swiveling around to take in the view from her window. All of a sudden the dejected feeling lifted like a fog to reveal deep, breathtaking blue skies.

Just like the blue of his eyes.

She smiled and when she reached her office, Mac turned in the chair at the sound of her door closing with a snap. Her breath caught in her throat. In the short time she'd been away from him, she'd forgotten the sheer appeal of the man. He sat nonchalantly, so completely male, so powerfully sexual without any effort. His eyes held no apology. His gaze said he had every right to be there, confident in her acceptance. As if he knew she found his calm self-assurance not only a challenge but a huge turn-on, as well.

She could only imagine what he had in mind for her, but she was ready for anything. Unable to resist the pull of his charisma, she traversed the space dividing them and settled into his lap, the anticipation curling low in her stomach. His thighs were firm and muscular beneath her bottom, and the leather of his pants was smooth against her bare legs in an arousing way.

He offered her a chance to be bold and daring in a safe and sexy way. After all, if she intended to get herself a bad boy, the least she could do was enjoy him for as long as possible.

Slipping one arm around his neck, she sent her hand over the soft cotton T-shirt covering his tight abs and met his gaze. This close, she could feel the rise and fall of his wide, muscular chest, see the hot desire in his gold-flecked blue eyes and smell the musky, heady scent of his skin.

He placed his hand on her thigh. The warmth of his touch acted like a branding along the flesh he touched.

"Kiss me," he said simply.

6

What floats your boat?

a. charm,
b. flirting,
c. a smart mind,
d. a smart mouth
                    —Excerpt from Who's Your Hottie? *quiz,*
                                        SPICE *magazine*

HE WAITED FOR her to act. She could only guess from the short time that she'd been with him he wasn't a man who'd let a challenge go uncontested.

After a lifetime of being sensible and practical, she was more than ready to treat herself to a little excitement and adventure with a man who knew all about walking on the wild side.

She bent her head and took his mouth, moving her lips over his in a sweet, firm movement. With a soft moan, she deepened the kiss and felt his response in the way he pressed into her open mouth.

She'd craved this kind of an experience for so long, eager to accept and savor whatever he had to offer. And she wanted to make sure he understood that she would be up for whatever he had in mind, and she wasn't about to let him take the lead in everything.

She cupped the back of his head, her fingers caressing his thick, silky hair.

Abruptly, he ended the kiss and buried his face against her throat, his breathing coming as fast and ragged as her own.

"Damn," he muttered, the one word explaining exactly how fiery and intense their attraction was.

She laughed huskily, knowing just how muddled he felt.

"I second that," she said trying to hang on to a coherent thought.

He lifted his head from the crook of her neck, his lashes half-mast and a sinful grin in place. "Contrary to what you believe, I didn't come here to throw you across your desk, hike up your skirt around your waist, and get between your thighs."

"Why did you come to my office at 3:00 in the afternoon then? Already my Monday is so much better."

"To entice you to something special I think you will like very much." He caressed her cheek with the back of his hand. "If we don't leave now, we'll be late."

Her cheeks warmed at his blatantly sexual statement, and while temptation beckoned, other more immediate responsibilities demanded her attention——the kind of duty and obligation that took precedence over her desire for Mac.

"Late for what?"

"You told me to make it a surprise." He leaned over and put his mouth against the sensitive shell of her ear and whispered. *"Surprise."*

A wonderful sensation cascaded through her. "You're right. I did, but I thought we were meeting tonight."

"Surprise again. I couldn't wait. After I heard your sweet voice over the phone, I just had to see you." Slowly he lifted his gaze to hers. "And just for the record, that kiss was hotter than hell. I like it when a woman knows what she wants, and isn't afraid to go after it."

The compliment boosted her confidence in a way nothing had in a long time, and she couldn't resist flashing him a quick grin. "Thank you." She slid from his lap and straightened her skirt, doing her best to smooth out her appearance and regain her composure.

He stood, too, and grimaced as he adjusted the noticeable bulge straining against the fly of his jeans. Then he reached into his pocket and pulled out his keys. "Let's go," he whispered.

"But..." she started to protest.

He moved directly in front of her and clasped her upper arms in his big hands, his eyes direct and darkly sensual. Pulling her to his muscular frame, he kissed her—a hot, deep act of possession that left her weak-kneed and light-headed.

Once he released her, she skimmed her tongue along her lower lip, loving the arousing taste of him and his aggressive nature. Both thrilled her. "Okay, so where are we going?"

"Oh, no. You're not finding out that easily," he said, most definitely staking a claim on her and letting her know he was a man who took what he wanted—sometimes without asking. "Remember what I said when we first met. Spontaneity is my middle name."

Anytime, anywhere. She read the tantalizing message in his eyes and accepted his challenge. Spontaneity and impulsive acts, she could handle. She'd gone looking for them and found them in that motorcycle shop and in Mac. After her fiasco in the conference room, she needed to do something out of the ordinary, maybe get back her equilibrium. She intended to add some spice and excitement to her current, sensible, straitlaced life.

Skipping work was something she hadn't done since she'd joined Waterford Scott, but it would only be a couple hours and she justified it by remembering that she had worked through her lunch hour.

She wouldn't mind if some of his personality rubbed off on her. The confidence he exuded. She bet he never had a problem standing up for himself.

MAC WAS LOSING IT over this woman, but he couldn't help himself. After his meeting downtown had ended early, he wanted to see Laurel and he didn't want to wait until tonight. The impulse of the act of changing his clothes and going over to her place of business wasn't lost on him. He knew how Laurel would see it and it worked in his favor.

As he escorted her out of her office and waited patiently while she told her assistant that she was taking the rest of the day off, his mind went back to that kiss. Damn, the woman had a wicked mouth on her. She'd just about burned him up in the fireball of her embrace, staking a claim on him that said their agreed-upon affair would be a balance between them and filled with amazing sensual experiences. Lots of hot, satisfying sex in any way that turned them both on.

All of a sudden this playing at being a bad boy wasn't such a bad thing. He was enjoying stepping out of his own straid character and walking on the wild side with such an exciting woman. Slipping into his bad-boy persona was a little easier than he thought it would be. It meant breaking rules, but he found that he liked his spur-of-the-moment escapades with Laurel.

Down in the street, the late afternoon sunshine was warm. She stopped when she saw the sleek gray-blue car.

"Wow."

He'd decided to drive his sports car, even though he knew Laurel would question how he could afford such a car. "It was a gift from my uncle who owns a dealership on the Upper East Side of Manhattan." At least he didn't have to lie. It was the truth and he rarely drove it, but he wanted to take her to her surprise in style and comfort.

She stood there for a moment looking at the car. Giving him a wary glance, her eyes thoughtful, she asked. "Mac, where were you born?"

"Here in Manhattan at Lenox Hill Hospital."

"Lenox Hill? That's located on the Upper East Side."

He looked away. "Uh-huh."

"That's interesting, since that's such a ritzy part of town."

He shrugged. "Where were you born?"

"In Brooklyn. It was way before my father was a Wall Street mogul."

"Modest beginnings, huh?"

"Yes, and you born at Lenox Hill. It's really strange."

"I'm not all that interesting."

"Really? I'd say that you are. I like the myriad of conflicting personalities. The tough-don't-need-anyone biker and the observant, sensitive guy who drops by my office to give me a surprise. I'd say you're a good guy in a bad-boy package."

He refrained from saying anything else that might have him eating shoe leather.

"The car is really nice though," was all she said, but he saw the unease in her eyes.

And damn if the guilt didn't come crashing down on him again. Mac was doing the best that he could to keep everything as close to the truth as possible. But showing her this car may have been a tactical error and he hated the fact that he had to worry about everything he did and everything he said.

Trying to let the guilt go and enjoy the excursion, he lost himself in maneuvering through traffic.

When they parked, she turned to him and said, "The Met? But what are we doing here? It's not a place I would expect you to take me."

She seemed pensive and not as excited as he'd expected her to be. "Oops there honey, your stereotyping is showing," he said, his tone gently chiding.

She looked sheepish. "I didn't mean to imply that you weren't aware of cultural events. I just thought you'd take me to a place that was...racy, dangerous even."

"No offense taken, and racy...and dangerous are good, but I don't consider the Met to be boring."

"True."

He looked at his watch and took her hand. "Come on we're going to be late."

LAUREL HADN'T been here since before her mother's death. She just couldn't identify why she felt...anxious. This had always been one of her favorite places. It could be that she was afraid that it would be too hard to be in the one building her mother spent so much time in. But she wasn't sure that was it.

Mac's hand was warm and tight around hers and she liked the way her palm fit against his. Her small fingers wrapped around the back of his big hand for comfort. She felt a little bit better.

Laurel didn't know what to make of this man. He was such an enigma. Hot black leather and the cerebral Met? The two didn't seem to mesh. But he obviously had such a rich personality. And what was it with the sports car? It fit him to a T, but she wondered about his roots. Lennox Hill hospital was definitely the place wealthy people went to have their babies. Maybe Mac's car-dealership uncle paid for Mac's mother to have her baby at that hospital. What did she know?

He took her through the museum to the Grace Rainey Rogers Auditorium. She pulled him to a stop when she saw the sign outside: Melanie Graham, consultant for design and architecture, Department of Modern Art, MMA, Art Deco: Form and Functionality—Jacques-Emile Ruhlmann, Monday, 4:00 p.m.

"You couldn't possibly have known that this is my favorite furniture designer."

"I guessed that he might be important, since he was your mother's favorite. Something may have rubbed off there."

There was a small silence; then Laurel met Mac's ardent gaze. It was as if he looked into her soul and saw

the need there, the desire to take what she had been exposed to her whole life and create. Try to capture, at
least, in her own small way the brilliance of some of
the art deco designers and craftsmen.

Something she couldn't hope to do. She didn't have
that much talent.

A host of feelings nailed Laurel right in the chest,
and she shifted against them. The words wouldn't
come, but the feelings were there, potent, catching her
off-guard. How had he done that? She couldn't believe
that he'd been so observant the night he spent at her
brownstone.

"Hey, babe. Everything okay?" he asked and she
nodded even though those feelings in her chest refused to budge. "It's just that you are so intuitive,
that's all."

"I thought you'd enjoy this lecture and exhibition."

"I will. Very much. Thank you."

"You looked like you were having a bad day back
there at the office."

"I was. Until you showed up."

"Boss riding your butt?"

"Yes."

"Why?"

"You know. I'm not really sure. I was promoted last
month to senior analyst and ever since I took the job, I
feel that Mr. Herman has it in for me. I don't understand
why he promoted me, if he feels that I can't do the job."

"Did you ask him?"

"No."

"Why not?"

"I don't know. I don't do very well with confrontations. I was just coming back from a staff meeting where my boss took away a really big account."

"What do you want to do about it?"

Of all the things he could have said, nothing could have thrown her more. Her father and brother always tried to fix everything for her, but not Mac. His confidence in her bolstered her even more.

He caught her under the chin, forcing her to look at him. When he saw her eyes, his softened and he caught her by the neck and pulled her into his embrace—a warm, safe embrace. "Come on, Laurel," he cajoled. "I know you've thought about it."

Mac tucked his face down against hers and tightened his hold, then slowly rubbed his hand up and down her back.

She shivered and pressed herself against him, feeling on the edge of some serious feelings for this man. "I have. I want to get a new client and rub it in Mr. Herman's and Mark Dalton's faces," she responded in a firm, tight voice that even surprised her.

He hugged her tighter and laughed, "That's my girl."

She laughed, too, releasing a lot of tension in her chest. When she looked at him, at the spark of amusement in his eyes, she fell a little deeper in like with him. Laurel told herself that it would be stupid on her part to get involved with a guy like Mac. Temporary was written all over him and that's how she wanted him. Right? Right, she said firmly to herself. He was oh-so-charming though, the kind of charm that would make it very easy to fall in love with him.

"Do you have a plan, yet?" he asked.

She moved out of his embrace, trying desperately to keep some emotional distance. "No. Not yet."

"My brother Ted, he...er...told me about this big company he has as a client."

"What's the name of it?"

"Coyle and Hamilton."

"Wow. That would be big enough. Does Ted know if they're satisfied with their current accounting company?"

He turned to look at her, but dropped his gaze. "I think he said that they were looking for the best, that's why he was always trying to find bigger and better ways to serve them."

I guess it can't hurt to contact them," she said. "How do you know so much about corporate business?"

"I always go with my instincts. And it's always served me well in my...ah...life. I don't think it'd be any different for you."

"Good afternoon, ladies and gentlemen. Thank you for attending our lecture. Without further preamble, let me introduce to you our curator, Melanie Graham."

A lovely, blond woman came up to the podium. She set some notes down and spoke into the microphone. "Good afternoon. Thank you all for attending this lecture. Don't miss the exhibition here at the museum after my talk concludes.

"The nineteenth century arts and crafts movement concentrated on a return to good craftsmanship, plain design and high-quality materials. Later art nouveau introduced the concept that art was not confined to the fine arts but could also be applied to functional objects like furniture. After the First World War there were great social changes which influenced the kinds of furniture required. There was also an emphasis, for those who could afford it, on well-designed decorative furniture which also included a high degree of functionality.

"Amongst art deco designers there were two clear schools: The first was the direct inheritor of the two earlier movements. These designers concentrated on individual pieces made by highly skilled craftsmen and could only be bought by the very rich. On the other hand, some art deco designers sought to take advantage of mass production. These designers also tended toward a severely geometric look which emphasized the functionality of the object."

Mac stretched his arm across the back of her seat, curving his fingers along the nape of her neck. She shivered and tried to focus on the lecture.

Melanie's voice seemed to get more distant. "At the start of the art deco movement, furniture was based on traditional styles but opulence was the keynote. Exotic woods like amboyna were used and decoration incorporated materials like ivory. These were the objects that were designed as objects of fine art as well as for functionality. By the mid 1920s the taste for such flamboyant furniture was waning. Modern materials like chrome were incorporated into the designs and they become more geometric and streamlined. It was at this time that Rene Lalique was making glass panels to be used in the furniture."

He traced the soft skin of Laurel's throat with his thumb. It was a simple caress, but his touch and the way he treated her, elicited complicated feelings inside her. Ones she had a very tough time fighting.

Laurel closed her eyes, thoughts buzzing through her head as the woman's voice filled the auditorium.

She shifted closer to Mac, breathing in the scent of him. He slipped his hand into her unbound hair, letting it sift through his fingers. Resting her head on his shoulder, she released a soft sigh. She couldn't remember the last time one of her boyfriends had read her so well, or taken the time to observe her as thoroughly as Mac had.

She was truly impressed with him and partly dismayed. He seemed like two different sides of the same coin and she liked both sides very much. But that only complicated matters more since she was expecting her fling with him to be purely physical and not stimulating intellectually or rich with emotion. He'd surprised her once again.

Laurel opened her eyes and tried to concentrate on what Melanie was saying. "Jacques-Emile Ruhlmann is only one of the fine designers that we have on exhibition thanks to the generous donations of Anne Wilks Malone. He is considered to be the premier art deco furniture designer. His furniture making techniques were flawless. Joints could barely be discerned, giving pieces the impression of being made from a single carved section of wood. For all its elegance, the furniture was designed to be used and to be comfortable. Form and design served to enhance the use of the furniture."

Laurel shifted at the sound of her mother's name. She was swamped by the enormous sense of pride that she had for her mother's achievements and humbled by her mother's dedication. She had been relentless in her procurement of furniture that showcased the beginning movement of art deco.

Melanie's eyes met Laurel's in the crowd and Laurel suddenly wanted to be anywhere but here.

Through the rest of the lecture, Mac was a solid, tempting pressure against her side.

Thank you ladies and gentlemen for your attention," Melanie said in closing. "Please be sure to visit our fine exhibition in the Anne Wilks Malone Memorial Art Deco Wing."

Melanie immediately came down from the podium and called Laurel's name.

Laurel stopped and faced the curator, her palms suddenly clammy.

"Laurel, it's so good to see you."

Laurel smiled and turned to Mac. "Let me introduce you to Mac Hayes."

Melanie acknowledged him with a smile and a handshake. She said, "I'm so flattered that you attended my talk, Laurel. We don't see you at the museum much anymore."

"I've been very busy," Laurel said, her stomach beginning to churn.

"Your mother was such a wonderful, delightful woman. I still can't believe that she's gone," she paused and sighed. "How is that wonderful memorial you're planning coming along?"

"It's stalled somewhat. We just found out that Christie's booked a big auction on the same night as ours, and they can't move it or cancel it."

"Oh, I'm so sorry to hear that. Please, let me know if there's anything I can do to help."

"I will."

They turned to go and Mac slipped his hand into Laurel's. "You okay?"

"Yes, I'm fine."

"You don't seem fine. Did the curator upset you?"

"No, really. I'm fine."

"Okay, if you say so. Why don't we go out front and get something to eat?"

"Hot dogs with the works," Laurel said hopefully, trying desperately to act like she was fine. She was suddenly feeling feelings she didn't want to feel, that elusive sense of wanting something. . .she wished she knew what. The thickness in her chest climbed higher.

"A woman after my own heart."

They made their way to the massive entrance to the Met and found a hot dog vendor. After Mac paid for the heavily laden dogs, they sat down on the stairs to eat them.

"Did you know that in recent months, residents of that building across the street want the Met to stop their plans to renovate? Can you believe that?" Mac said, gesturing to the impressive building.

Laurel felt some of the tension in her release at the sound of Mac's soothing voice. She was here with him and that was enough for now. She'd sort her feelings out later. "Some people don't have any vision. They probably think that they'll get their million dollar view of Central Park cut off." Her eyes scanned the snarled traffic on Fifth Avenue and watched trucks delivering things to the museum.

She could remember the day they had moved everything from the attic and clogged rooms of their big mansion in Westchester County. Her mother had been as giddy as a schoolgirl and her infectious sense of humor had rubbed off on everyone around her. She even had her stoic father in stitches. The memory made her smile and the rest of the tension drained out of her.

A truck rumbled by interrupting her view and drawing her out of the memory. Fumes rose from grates in the sidewalk. A tour bus pulled up and a large group of noisy, excited visitors congregated on the steps. In the street, Laurel watched a crowd of young kids goofing around, and farther away there was an old, disheveled man playing a flute in front of a case of coins. This was New York at its finest. Truly, some people just didn't appreciate it.

Mac looked at his watch. "Ready to catch the exhibit?"

"Yes. I can't wait."

AFTER THREE HOURS of looking at the finest pieces of art deco furniture in one collection, Mac walked hand and hand with Laurel through the hall to reach his car, wishing the day wouldn't have to end.

Mac stopped at the entrance to the wing which included a large rotunda with pictures of Laurel's mother on the wall, along with numerous awards for her work in the arts.

"Laurel, I have an idea."

"What?"

"Hear me out. You could line up chairs right along here and put the podium there. The furniture could be set up down the hall to be showcased."

Laurel looked at him and then she looked at the space. Tears filled her eyes.

"It was just a thought. Damn, did I make you cry?"

She shook her head and wrapped her arms around him. "What a fitting place to have my mother's memorial. I should have thought of it myself."

He held her, her body warm and soft against his.

Somehow this had been a trying day for her, but he wasn't sure why. He wanted to know, but each time he'd tried to broach the subject, Laurel had put him off. Either she wasn't sure herself, or she didn't want to share her thoughts with him.

"Now all I have to do is call one hundred and fifty people and let them know there's been a change of venue."

"Need some help with that?"

Her gaze locked on his face. A startled look appeared in her eyes. "Mac, it's going to be a couple of late nights for me. After the calling, I have the catering to handle, the flowers, and all the designers who are donating the furniture. You have to work tomorrow. It's very kind of you, but you don't have to."

He knew what she was saying. He was violating his bad-boy persona, but he didn't care. Getting into her personal space was too enticing for him to give ground now. He was afraid if he didn't push a little too hard, she wouldn't let him in ever. She'd end the affair and damn if he didn't already have too much invested to back off now. He realized that she saw him as a temporary stud. It was his choice to play this game and now he was caught in it. But he didn't have to play by Laurel's rules. He could make up his own as he went along. "You have work tomorrow, too. I didn't offer because I had to, Laurel. I want to help you."

Laurel studied him, her dark eyes suddenly unreadable. Mac prepared for another argument and even for her to tell him no. She didn't need his help.

Instead, she bumped his hip and said "So," her voice deceptively casual, "just what do you want for this help you're offering?"

Now she was trying to pass it off as sexual and, therefore, meaningless. He could play along if it would make her feel better.

He dredged up an off-center smile, injecting a touch of humor into his tone. "You must have me mixed up with some other sex-crazed maniac."

"Oh, I don't think so, but I guess you'll have to do," she said in a long-suffering tone.

"Oh, I will?" he replied, catching her around the waist and swinging her. Her laughter echoed off the marble walls. Off balance, she fell into him and they laughed even harder as they fell to the floor, her on top of him.

Laughing, his whole body going on full alert, he slid his arms around her hips. "Way to go, Gracie," he murmured needing to taste those smiling lips.

"Hey, don't get mouthy. You had a hand in this, too."

"So I did."

Laurel stared at him and then managed a wry smile. "You are bad."

"And you love it."

"Yes, I do." She looked down into his face and he felt something shift, crackle, and expand in his chest. This woman was getting under his skin faster than stocks could plummet and crash.

"Come on," she said getting to her feet, showing that she felt that shift in the air every bit as much as he did. "Let's go take Melanie Graham up on her offer to help...and book this beautiful rotunda."

MAC MANEUVERED the car through the heavy stop-and-go traffic, he took Laurel's hand and pressed it against his thigh, covering it with his own. Her only response was to turn her hand palm-up, lacing her fingers through his. When he glanced at her, she was sitting with her head tipped back against the headrest, her eyes closed, as if absorbing the invigorating rush of the wind. She looked serene and relaxed, but he could see the slight tension along her jawline, as though she had her teeth clenched.

Twilight had settled in by the time they reached her brownstone and he pulled to the curb. Laurel took his hand in hers.

Inside her brownstone, she kept ahold of Mac's hand and brought him into her living room.

"Let me get the list," she said as she disappeared into the kitchen.

She returned a few moments later with a sheaf of papers. She handed a few to him and kept some for herself. Giving him the house phone, she pulled her cell out of her purse.

Hours later, Mac disconnected his last call. It was simply too late to make any more. He looked at Laurel who had fallen asleep on her side of the couch. He slipped his arms under her and headed for the stairs. Up in her dimly lit room, he stripped her and tucked her into bed.

After a moment of debate, he shucked his clothes and climbed in with her. Pulling her against him, feeling as if he was in sheer heaven, he closed his eyes.

Only to have them fly open immediately. Her soft hand slid down his body, over his buttocks, just a slow caressing glide as if she was savoring the shape of his muscles, the texture of his skin.

He met her gaze in the dim room, her gaze was direct and she looked pretty wide awake to him. "Thank you," she said softly. "I'm sorry I fell asleep on you."

"No problem," he managed, sliding his arms under her, kissing the curve of her shoulder as he shifted his hips between her thighs. Her breath caught, and she clutched him tighter. He moved his hips again, deliberately maximizing body contact, and there was another sharp intake of breath.

She rolled over and fumbled with the nightstand drawer. When she moved back, she made short work of slipping on the condom.

Shifting until he was on top of her, he braced his weight on his elbows and used his knees to open her legs wider. Thrusting inside, he held himself immobile. Grasping her face between his hands, he commanded huskily, "Look at me, Laurel."

He heard her swallow; then she caressed her hands down his spine to his buttocks, kneading them with hard, firm strokes. Holding her gaze, he slowly flexed his hips again, rocking hard against her, and she arched her neck and closed her eyes, the pulse point in her throat beating erratically.

Watching her face, he moved again, and he could feel the tension mount in her. And he knew. He had an intuitive sense about her delectable body. She was already close.

His fingers tangling in her hair, he gripped her head.

"Look at me," he said softly. "I want you to look at me."

As if it cost her an unbearable effort, she did as he asked, her eyes glazed and dilated. "Stay with me, babe," he whispered; then he moved again, and she tried to arch her neck, but he held her still. "Stay with me."

His gaze locked on hers, he slowly moved against her, in her, maximizing the pressure against her. She clutched his arms, her eyes glazing even more, and she drew up her knees alongside his hips, her body arching with tension. His breathing turning erratic, he continued to move, watching her respond, her tightness driving him on. She gripped his arms, a desperate look turning her eyes black; then, on a fragmented moan, she twisted her head, her whole body arching, and he felt her contract hard around him, her release shuddering through her. Feeling as if something wild and unbearably beautiful had been set loose in his chest, he closed his eyes and gathered her up in a fierce embrace, experiencing feelings that went far beyond the sexual.

It took several moments for her to come back down to earth and he grasped her, holding her tight and secure. Finally she shifted under him, letting go a long shaky breath.

Her arms locked around his shoulders, she buried her face against his neck, her whole body trembling. "Oh, no. Mac. You didn't...."

Experiencing a rush of tenderness, he smiled. "I had too much fun watching you come and let me tell you. You're making my ego big."

She tightened her arms around him, still trembling a little. "That's not the only thing that's big about you."

He grinned.

She pushed on his shoulders and made him roll over. "It's one of the things I so like about you," she said softly. To prove her point, she reached down and curled her hand around his erection and stroked upward.

Mac lost any teasing comeback he might have had on his lips.

Unable to hold back the rampant male instincts firing his blood or to resist the hot female invitation in her eyes, he curled his hand around her neck and pulled her sweet mouth down to his. Her lips parted beneath the coaxing pressure of his mouth, and his tongue swept inside, slow and teasing, then gradually taking possession of her mouth in a deep, wet, ravenous kiss that was unmistakable in its carnality and sexual intent.

Shifting her body, she took him to the hilt and he gasped and groaned.

She met him movement for movement. Plunging in deep, he grasped her hips, holding himself inside her, his biceps bunching with the exquisite strain of holding himself immobile. Her fingers curled in his hair, tugging so hard it was painful. He gritted his teeth against the intense pain and pleasure of holding back. Then she cried out his name and his mouth took the sound so deep inside, he let himself go. He thought he could die right now and never regret it.

She collapsed on his chest and for a moment he held her smiling. He felt pure happiness.

"Why are you smiling?"

"Just because." Running his hand up and down her back, he rested his head against hers, liking the feel of her damp, naked body against his. Then he felt the brush of Laurel's long eyelashes as she closed her eyes.

He continued to stroke her back. After a few moments he felt her body go slack, and he knew she had dropped off to sleep, which gave him a certain amount of satisfaction. She felt comfortable enough to fall asleep on him. He shifted her to the soft mattress, releasing a contented sigh. Drawing his arm around her, he closed his eyes, his throat suddenly tight.

He hoped like hell he wasn't messing up this relationship by not telling her who he was.

MAC STOOD AT her bedroom door watching her sleep. He wasn't sure why he woke up—maybe it was because the room had turned cold, maybe it was the soft drip, drip, drip of the faucet in the bathroom. Or maybe because he was in her house and unaccustomed to waking up here. But whatever it was, he was too awake now, with no blurred edges from a deep sleep or half-forgotten dreams. The fading sky that preceded dawn was illuminating the room and as it brightened he could see more of Laurel.

She was sleeping on her side, facing him, one leg drawn up, her breathing deep and even. The windows had been left open all night, and the room was chilly, cooled by the breeze full of the scents of Manhattan along with the sounds of a waking city—blaring horns, squealing brakes, and slamming car doors.

He sipped his coffee and took in the brightening room.

It had been too dim the previous night for him to notice or appreciate the décor. The giant bed. The intricate furniture. Even the midnight-blue walls made him think of cooling water and he felt himself begin to relax. Colorful, erotic abstract art hung on the walls in pea green and dark-blue colors. Pea green wasn't a color that he would have thought would have meshed well with the multicolored carpet, but it did.

Her sanctuary was worlds apart from the conventional look of her living room. For a moment he just stood there and took it all in. His curiosity about Laurel went up a notch, a woman who had deep facets. Why was her bedroom so very different from the rest of her house?

Bracing his weight against the doorjamb he finished the coffee in his cup in one gulp. He walked across the bedroom and set the cup on the nightstand. He ran his hand down her bare arm then he reached over, tugged the sheet loose and drew it over her. He watched her sleep for a long time, until parts of his body started sending him messages that had nothing to do with sleep and everything to do with the woman beside him. For an instant he indulged in a fantasy about easing her onto her back and slipping inside her while she slept, giving her a special wake-up call.

But he had to leave and get home to change. He had back-to-back client meetings today, specifically with Kevin Coyle. Still, he lingered, finally he sat on the bed and smoothed his hand over her face and hair.

Laurel opened her eyes and smiled, "Hey there," she said groggily. "You leaving?"

"Yeah, got to get to work. Tuesdays are one of my busiest days. Good luck with Coyle and Hamilton. There's half a pot of coffee downstairs."

"He even makes coffee. I think I'm in love." She sighed. Thanks."

Mac's stomach lurched. He knew she was just making an offhand remark meant to be a joke. So why did his heart leap and want to do cartwheels? He got up and headed for the door, but stopped and turned when she called his name.

"Thanks again for last night. The phone calling, I mean."

"I know what you meant and you're welcome." Damn, he thought as he left her brownstone, he would make a million phone calls for one of those soft, tender looks she'd given him.

He was a goner.

7

What hottie ride do you find sexy?

a. motorcycle,
b. Jeep,
c. Jaguar,
d. limo

> —*Excerpt from* Who's Your Hottie? *quiz,*
> SPICE *magazine*

LAUREL GOT TO WORK a little late, but she couldn't seem to care. Unlike Mac, Tuesdays were not all that busy for her. She wondered if mechanics had busy days because they booked a lot of work on Tuesdays or if they seemed to have more customers that day. It seemed an odd statement for him to make.

She walked into her office and found Mark sitting at her desk. He swiveled around in her chair and as usual gave her one of those sneering looks.

"What do you think you're doing?" Laurel demanded.

"I needed a file and your phone rang, so I answered it and took care of the problem."

Laurel just reacted. "Who do you think you are?"

"I'm just taking care of business. I was here on time."

Anger surged through her like lightning through oak. She closed her eyes to gather her composure. "If I remember correctly, I'm your supervisor and, as such, you will treat me with respect. No more undermining my authority or any more rude comments. If you have a grievance, you can take it up with Mr. Herman. Is that clear?"

Mark's eyes narrowed and he rose from her desk. Walking up to her, he invaded her personal space. As in the past, he used his height as an intimidation and it had always worked. But now Laurel, empowered by her relationship with Mac and her ability to demand want she wanted from him, found a core of steel inside herself. She realized she could handle a hundred Mark Daltons.

She raised her chin and kept eye contact with him.

"Fine, Laurel, but you have to know that this job should have been mine because I worked for it. I can't say the same for you."

"I'm sorry that you're disappointed you didn't get this job, but it doesn't have anything to do with me."

"You think so? I'd ask Mr. Herman about that if I were you."

"I will, but in the meantime, you will not enter my office without my permission or answer my phone. You will address me in a professional manner. If you don't, I'll speak to Mr. Herman."

He went out of her office and slammed the door. Setting her briefcase down on her desk, she allowed herself a little smile of satisfaction, yet the nagging question of what exactly he was hinting at bothered her. To hell with it. She really didn't have time to worry about Mark Dalton and his bruised ego and nasty insinuations.

After settling herself in her chair, she booted up her computer and Googled Coyle and Hamilton. It was time to do her homework and hook a big fish and prove to Mr. Herman and Mark Dalton that her promotion was justified.

She spent the morning putting together an initial proposal using a concept she called unitedthinking, pulling together four aspects of Waterford and Scott's philosophies on how they conducted business. When she was ready, she picked up the phone and dialed.

"Coyle and Hamilton."

"Yes, please connect me with Natasha Gold, your Chief Financial Officer."

"One moment."

There were a couple of clicks and then Natasha's assistant came on the line. After Laurel stated her business, she was put through.

"This is Natasha Gold."

"Good morning. I am calling from Waterford Scott, we're a full-service accounting firm…."

"Yes, I've heard of your firm, Ms. Malone, but what would you have to offer us?"

"Waterford Scott serves many of the leading businesses in every sector on which we focus. Those businesses value our rigorous, practical approach, characterized by a detailed understanding of individual client issues and by deep industry knowledge and experience.

"We invest significant resources in building and sharing industry expertise to help us serve clients to the fullest extent of our ability.

"I would very much like to meet with you to propose

an innovative way of doing business. We here at Waterford Scott believe in a concept we call unitedthinking."

"This unitedthinking sounds interesting. We're actually in the market for an accounting firm at this time."

"I'd like to meet with you, give you information about my company during a preliminary meeting, then, perhaps present a full-scale presentation to Mr. Coyle and Ms. Hamilton."

"Let me see, I could squeeze you in today say at two-thirty this afternoon."

"That would be wonderful."

"I'll expect you then."

Laurel hung up the phone and got up and danced around her desk. She could just kiss Mac for giving her the inside scoop that the company was looking for a new firm. The right place at the right time.

Giving herself another moment of satisfaction, she settled herself back into her office chair and started to prepare for her meeting.

Working diligently through the morning, Laurel was satisfied that she had the beginning of a good plan for her meeting. She ate a sandwich at her desk and called the caterer to let them know that the food for the auction event should be delivered to the Met and would be set up in the Grace Rogers Auditorium. Next, she called and said the same to the florist, directing them to the rotunda. She then called a few more attendees to alert them that the auction had moved locations.

Once her hour was up, she went back to work on her proposal and put the finishing touches on it at two o'clock. Gathering up her notes and her proposal, she put everything in her briefcase. Stepping outside her office, she told her assistant she was leaving for a meeting downtown and wouldn't be back.

Down in the street she hailed a cab and sat back in the seat to relax. Normally, her stomach would be churning and although Laurel was nervous, it was a good nervousness.

She dug into her purse to look for her lipstick. Her hand encountered a square object. With a frown, she grabbed it and pulled it out. Oh no, she'd forgotten to give Mac back his pocket PC. After all that he'd done for her yesterday, the least she could do was drop it off to Mac after her meeting. Hayes Cycles wasn't too far out of her way. Of course, she'd have the added bonus of seeing him all scruffy-looking again. Haley was right. He was very easy on the eyes.

Seeing him would also give her the opportunity to thank him again for his tip about Coyle and Hamilton.

When the cab approached 27th Street, Laurel caught a glimpse of a vacant storefront. As they passed, she craned her neck to keep the empty windows in sight. It would make such a perfect place for her to sell her furniture.

It had great display possibilities with the abundant large glass windows. The property was nestled in an area of craft and specialty shops that would cater to the kind of people who would be interested in her projects. It had a large area in the back for parking and loading delivery trucks.

She sighed. Where the heck had that thought come from? Not once had she thought her stuff good enough to sell. Sure, what she made she gave as gifts, but it brought her pleasure to know that people were enjoying her pieces. Now that the idea was full blown, she couldn't seem to forget about it. Would anyone even be interested in her furniture? Mac sure liked the chair and table she'd done, but he could have just said that to be nice.

She had worked for Waterford Scott for five years and it was her intention to make partner. The fanciful thought of her having the guts to give up her job and make furniture for a living was just that, fanciful.

AN HOUR AND A HALF LATER, giddy with her success, Laurel caught another cab and headed for the dealership. Natasha Gold had been thrilled with her proposal, impressed by the services of Waterford Scott and had indicated she wished to set up a meeting two weeks later for a full-scale presentation.

When the cab pulled up to the dealership, Laurel paid the driver and got out. Feeling light as air and excited about seeing Mac, she opened the door and walked in.

Tyler was helping a customer, so she wandered close to the glass door that separated the showroom from the repair shop.

"You looking for Mac?"

"Yes. I really need to give him something that he left at my place."

Tyler shook his head. "Ah...he didn't show up. I don't know where he is."

"Look, could you give me his address? I really need to see him and he won't mind. Truly. I have to return something to him."

"I don't know." He paused. "Are you sure he won't mind?"

"Mac? His middle name is spontaneity. I think he'd love to see me. Besides, I have something he wants."

"MAC, SHE'S ON HER WAY to my apartment. Get your ass over there," Tyler blurted.

"What?" Mac couldn't grasp the meaning of the words right away. Was she on her way to his apartment?

"Laurel. She says she has to give you something you left at her place. It's important. I don't know what it's about. I gave her my address. You don't want her going to your loft. It'll give everything away. All she has to do is see your place and you're history."

"Oh, God. My pocket PC. I forgot all about it."

"You forgot? This girl really must be addling your brain."

"Has she opened it?"

"I don't know."

"Did she seem upset?"

"No. I guess she wanted to make sure you got it back. Mac, get going!"

He told Sherry he was late for a meeting and was leaving for the day.

When he got to Tyler's place he pelted up the stairs and used his spare key to let himself in. The moment the door closed behind him, he started stripping. Tripping on his pants, he ran to his brother's bedroom. He shoved his thousand-dollar Armani suit under the bed and ran for the shower.

Jumping in, he turned on the spray, crying out when the cold water hit him. He frantically adjusted the knobs and when the temperature was right, he washed the hair gel out of his hair.

He heard the knocking as soon as he shut off the water. Grabbing a towel and wrapping it around his waist, he ran for the bedroom.

"Just a minute," he yelled.

He dried off as best he could and slipped on a pair of sweatpants and a Harley-Davidson T-shirt he found in Tyler's drawer.

Blowing out a frustrated breath, he decided that the first chance he got, he was going to punch his brother as hard as he could.

He opened the door and there she was, dressed in a black pantsuit of obvious quality with a gold blouse peeking from between the lapels. The sight of her hit him like a runaway truck. Maybe he would hold off on punching his brother.

"Mac," Laurel said softly.

He backed away from her. He suspected he'd always be caught by her eyes.

"How did you know where to find me?"

"Tyler told me. Please don't be mad at him."

"I'm not mad at him." He smiled. "I'm happy you're here." He just wished it wasn't under false pretenses and that his brother's apartment was his own. Guilt, sharp as a dagger, stabbed through him. The longer that he played out this deception, the more he wondered if he was going to lose Laurel in the end. How tolerant would she be when he confessed? Maybe he should tell her now.

"I have to admit that I could have waited until later to give you back your property, but I wanted to see you." She pulled his pocket PC out of her purse and handed it to him. Mac set it down on Tyler's hall table. "I wanted to thank you again."

"For helping you call…."

She covered his mouth and kissed him tenderly. "No, for giving me that tip on Coyle and Hamilton. I got an appointment today with Natasha Gold."

"Who's she?"

"Chief financial officer."

"When?"

"Today at two o'clock. I went to the dealership after my meeting."

"That's great. What was the outcome?" Mac breathed a sigh of relief. He had left Coyle and Hamilton at one o'clock. He'd only missed Laurel by an hour. In hindsight, perhaps it hadn't been such a good idea to tell her about the company. All the more reason to tell her who he really was. He gathered his courage. As soon as she finished talking, he would tell her.

"She's asked me to put together a full-scale presentation for Kevin Coyle and Susan Hamilton in two weeks."

All at once he changed his mind. He wanted her to savor her triumph without darkening it with his confession. He could wait a little bit longer. He'd have to make sure that he was careful when he visited Coyle and Hamilton. He wouldn't want to cross paths with Laurel while she still thought he was Mac the biker.

"So, do you have plans for dinner?" he asked.

"I thought I would get something quick and make some more calls."

"How about something here and I'll help you make those calls.

LAUREL OPENED HER DOOR on Sunday morning, looking forward to another full day of sawdust and power tools. She barely kept herself from colliding with a well-muscled chest, encased in black leather.

"Great. You're dressed perfectly for Central Park."

"Central Park? Mac?" Laurel squeaked.

"Are you expecting someone else?"

She stepped back to look up at him, waiting for him to shift his gaze to hers. "I wasn't expecting anyone. I was going out." The truth of the matter was that she was thrilled he was here. Mac settled on one hip and cocked the other one in a sexy pose that did funny things to her insides. He was wearing tight black jeans and a white T-shirt, and his leather jacket, of course. He obviously hadn't shaved that morning; dark stubble shaded his jaw and cheeks, and his thick, sable hair was rumpled around his head. A wicked grin curved his lips, and his bright blue eyes sparkled with shameless purpose.

He looked disreputable, gorgeous, and ready and willing to commit a whole lot of sin.

Okay, so he wasn't a long-term guy, but the man was most definitely her every fantasy come to life. She'd already given herself permission to enjoy him for the time being and that was exactly what she intended to do.

"Where are you going, Laurel?"

She was on the verge of telling him, but changed her mind. She still didn't know him well enough. Sure they'd connected, but why blurt out her secret to a man she didn't expect would be around in a couple of months? She and Mac would burn out soon enough. It was better she keep some things to herself. "On errands, Mr. Nosy."

"I'm sorry. I didn't realize you'd be busy."

Laurel rolled her eyes. "Just like a guy. It's the weekend, Mac. I have more than enough to keep me busy."

To tell the truth she was a bit peeved that she hadn't heard from him. Granted she told him she was busy Wednesday night with the florist and Thursday night, she had to work late, but he hadn't contacted her on Friday night and Saturday he had to work. Now he had the nerve to show up on her doorstep.

"Well, look at you all sassy and tough." He gave her a hang-dog expression, turning his mouth down. "No Central Park?"

She gave him a cheeky grin. The man had charm in spades as her bad mood disintegrated like sugar in boiling water. "I guess my errands can wait," she said with a put upon sigh.

She closed and locked her door and followed him to the curb.

"When was the last time you went to Central Park?" he asked.

Laurel shrugged. "Well, I've never really taken the time to see much of the park at all."

"Typical New Yorker," Mac snorted.

"How about you?" she asked as she settled against him on his bike.

"I used to go with my parents. They loved the park, but I haven't been there in a while."

"What exactly are we going to do there?"

"Take a bike tour," Mac responded, firing up the Ducati.

"You really are full of surprises," she shouted over the wind.

"Is that a good thing?"

"Yes. It is."

A half hour later, Mac lead Laurel into the park and

when they reached the bike area, the tour guide assigned each of them a bike. The first stop was Strawberry Fields—the beautiful memorial to John Lennon.

The tour guide halted them with his hand up in the air and began to speak. "A cathedral of American elms provides the shade which protects the black-and-white tiled mosaic from the direct glare of the sun. A gift of Naples, Italy, it is a reproduction of a Pompeii mosaic and inscribed at its center is the word *Imagine*."

The memorial was fitting as John was a peaceful, introspective man. She'd only been a year old when the ex-Beatle had been gunned down in front of the Dakota, but she'd discovered the music when she'd been sixteen. She looked across the street at the apartment building.

"What a waste, huh?" Mac said.

"It sure was. He was an amazing musician. I couldn't get enough of the Beatles when I was a kid. I once played 'I Wanna Hold Your Hand' fifty times until my dad told me if I played that song one more time, he would break the CD in half. So I switched to 'She Loves Me.'"

Mac chuckled. "I was a Boss guy myself. Couldn't get enough of Springsteen. Although I was sorry about Lennon. I didn't discover the Beatles until I was eighteen, but I always thought John had the vision."

"He followed his dream and was always genuine. He never let anyone tell him who to be. My tastes run to Nine Inch Nails now."

Mac's eyebrows rose. "Interesting band for a high-class girl from Manhattan."

Laurel smiled. "They rock."

"I bet your parents hated that you listed to alternative bands."

The Reader Service™ — Here's how it works:

Accepting the free books places you under no obligation to buy anything. You may keep the books and gift and return the despatch note marked 'cancel'. If we do not hear from you, about a month later we'll send you 4 brand new books and invoice you just £3.05* each. That's the complete price - there is no extra charge for postage and packing. You may cancel at any time, otherwise every month we'll send you 4 more books, which you may either purchase or return to us - the choice is yours.

*Terms and prices subject to change without notice.

"My parents never knew. Do you think they would have let me keep those CDs? No way, my mother didn't allow anything in the house with profanity in it. I would have been grounded for a month and everything in my room would have been scrutinized."

"Wow. That's tough, Laurel."

She shrugged. "That's the way they were. Strict and demanding, but I turned out pretty good."

He nudged her with his shoulder. "I'll say."

The next stop on the tour was Shakespeare's Garden, then Belvedere Castle and finally The Jacqueline Kennedy Onassis Reservoir.

As they stood on the shore of the reservoir looking out at the great expanse where their tour took a momentary rest, Laurel realized how much she'd revealed to him without really meaning to. It was much too easy to talk to this man. Yet, he was guarded about the details of his own life. Laurel knew that she should keep away from personal questions, but she couldn't seem to help herself. They were from two different worlds and two very different philosophies. He seemed like he was a free spirit, yet he had a pocket PC. That incongruity in his personality tantalized her. Her curiosity got the better of her. Mac confused and bewildered her. "Do you skip out on work often?"

"What do you mean?"

"You weren't at the dealership on Tuesday. Your brother said that you didn't show up for work. I thought it was odd because you said you had a busy day."

He frowned and Laurel wondered if she was stepping on sacred ground.

"Keeping tabs on me, Laurel?"

"No. I just found it odd. That's all."

"What? You haven't blown off work?"

"No."

"Never?"

Laurel shot him a disgruntled look at the sound of his disbelief. "No, unless I was too sick to go. Suddenly that seems so pathetic to me. Why haven't I ever done that? Why hadn't I taken one day and gone shoe shopping or taken a trip to the Statue of Liberty?"

"You're too responsible, Laurel. That's why I'm the best thing that ever happened to you."

Her mood totally broke and she laughed, just as he intended her to do. He was much too cute for her sanity. She shouldn't allow herself to be amused by this rascal. She was a level-headed, practical sort of person, after all. But there was something about this side of Mac Hayes, something tempting, something conspiratorial. The gleam in his dark eyes pulled at her like a magnet. "And you're not responsible?"

"I didn't say that. It's that Tyler understands my moods and gives me space. I'm sure you don't get that at your uptight corporate job."

"That seems so irresponsible though. I mean, the least you could do was call and let him know that you're not going to show up."

"I need to do my own thing. Tyler's cool."

It was one aspect of being with this kind of man that caused red flags. Laurel liked letting go once in a while, especially in bed, but when it came to living up to the responsibilities that came with a job and relationships, she wouldn't skimp. It made her wonder if Mac had had any long-term relationships.

She did have a grudging admiration for the way he did his own thing and didn't worry about how the world viewed him. An innate confidence beamed out of his eyes until she felt soaked in it.

"I did enjoy the day."

"It's not over yet."

The tour guide called the short rest period over and they got on their bikes and made it back to where they had started.

Mac grabbed Laurel's hand and said, "Come with me. I have one more thing to show you."

They made their way into the park until they reached a small enclosure. Laurel gasped out loud with pleasure. "You're taking me to the carousel right in the middle of Central Park. I love it."

"At the risk of tarnishing my reputation, I cautiously say, me, too. My parents brought us here a lot. They really enjoyed the park."

He pulled her up to the circular platform and helped her straddle one of the horses. After a few moments, the horse started moving up and down and the carousel began to spin.

Laurel laughed out loud with a breathless anticipation as the ride started to go faster. She held on to the center pole. Her hair blew in the wind and it slapped her cheeks with massaging fingers.

The sky started to darken outside and they dimmed the lights in the building.

They rode the carousel until the manager called out, "last ride."

"Let's sit this one out," he said softly as he pulled her to one of the seats and dragged her down onto his lap. Her heels rested on the bench and she draped her arms around his neck.

Looking down into his face, her heart fluttered and started to beat fast.

There were times like this when she looked into his eyes and saw such depth, such charisma. At these times she wondered who he really was, devoid of the sexy clothes and the devil-may-care attitude. It seemed as if there was a different man there, one that she could love. Not just pretty packaging, but something so real that it would last forever.

Too bad he wasn't a forever kind of guy.

His hold tightened as the carousel began to move. Everyone had gone on and taken their rambunctious kids with them leaving her and Mac alone, except for the operator.

Refusing to analyze her conflicting emotions when they had no business being a part of her relationship with Mac, she tried to look away, but his soft words stopped her.

"Don't Laurel. I'm right here."

She swallowed. His dark blue eyes were open and gentle, and her reflection in the heated depths made her experience an out-of-body sensation.

Her hands tightened in the soft leather jacket he wore. "I always feel this breathless anticipation around you. As if you're my next breath."

He leaned forward, his mouth inches from hers, drawing on her desire like a silken cord that tightened with each pull of those mesmerizing eyes.

He pressed his mouth to hers, and she groaned as she met those sensual lips. His hand cupped the back of her head and he took her mouth, open and hot. His silky tongue thrust deep and tangled with hers.

She sunk into his embrace. The whirling of the carousel was nothing compared to the whirling of her senses from the taste and smell of Mac.

In her opinion, the ride was too short. Laurel felt like she was walking on air instead of the concrete. She slipped her hand into Mac's as they strolled together away from the carousel. Before long they were back at the curb and his bike. He released the helmets from the motorcycle and handed one to her.

"Where are you going to take me next? I think I touched heaven on that carousel."

He smiled that devastating smile and said, "Dinner sound good to you?"

She couldn't believe that she'd only met him a week ago. It felt as if she'd known him all her life. He'd offered her a bit of lighthearted fun after a long week of work and worry over her mother's memorial, a tempting escapade that spoke to a wilder, badder side of herself, which she had no idea she'd possessed until Mac brought it out in her.

She grinned, welcoming the rush of excitement infusing her veins. "I'm famished. Riding the carousel takes a lot out of you."

"I know this great place you'll love," he promised. I have something for you," he said as he opened the locked saddle bag on the back of the bike.

He pulled out a leather jacket and Laurel squealed in delight. "Mac, you shouldn't have done this, but I love it. The buckles and the chains are great."

He chuckled, pleased at her obvious pleasure. "I thought those would appeal to you."

He mounted the bike first and she climbed on behind, settling herself against him. He started the engine, and the whole bike rumbled to life, as did her nerve endings. Her pulse leaped, the vibrations arousing her body and tickling her already titillated senses.

She wrapped her arms around his waist. She leaned into the solid muscular strength of his back, bringing them intimately close and snug, and locked her fingers over his taut abdomen. He revved the high-powered engine once more, and off they went.

He drove along Broadway, taking her past the people-packed, sky-high center of New York City—Times Square. As many as one thousand people in an hour crossed the pedestrian island that sat between 45th and 46th Streets where Broadway and 7th Avenue intersected. Laurel craned her neck as the one-hundred-foot billboard flashed by. At night, the sights were incredible in the midst of the city, a mesmerizing combination of endless momentum and unstoppable light. Sitting on the back of the motorcycle, with the wind caressing her face, Laurel felt exhilarated, unrestrained, with a sense of freedom that had eluded her most of her life. She embraced the feeling, and Mac, and enjoyed the invigorating sensations rippling through her.

Before long he was turning down the street that led to Pier 84 and the trendy Hell's Kitchen area where there was an abundance of shops, art galleries, music and restaurants.

He parked the motorcycle and helped her off. It took her a moment to regain her footing since her legs were shaking from the vibrations of the engine. She took off her helmet and ran her hands through her hair. Glancing at him, she couldn't resist dragging her hands through his hair to tame it and to connect with him.

His eyes softened and he cupped her cheek giving her a quick kiss.

She glanced out at the pier as realization dawned. "I haven't been here in a while. It sure has changed."

"I come here often," he said as they walked across 46th Street between Eighth and Ninth Avenues to find "Restaurant Row," a block of eateries that catered to theatergoers. "The food is excellent and in the summer there are festivals."

He came here often? In the theater district? "I wouldn't have thought that you would frequent their part of the city, let alone enjoy going to festivals," she said.

"Ah...well. What can I say, the food is good."

Puzzled at his hesitant answer and curious about the nervous look in his eye, she stopped on the sidewalk and said, "Are you worried that we'll meet someone you know here, like a woman?"

He gave her hand an affectionate squeeze. "No. I'm not worried about that, Laurel. It's stereotypical to think that just because I ride a bike and fix motorcycles I'm a caveman when it comes to anything else."

She tipped her head, regarding him speculatively. "You're absolutely right. That would be like you expecting me to know all about opera because I come from upper Manhattan. To tell you the truth, the quirks in your character only make you more appealing."

He dropped an impulsive kiss on her lips, which left

her yearning for a deeper, longer embrace. "If I make another stupid comment like that," she offered, "you have my permission to point out any of my many flaws."

"You do have this annoying habit..."

"Hey," she interrupted, punching his arm. "I said 'if I make another comment.'"

Mac chuckled.

"Laurel? Is that you, my dear."

Laurel froze at the sound of Mrs. Foster's voice. She turned toward the elderly woman and forced a smile.

"Mrs. Foster. How are you?"

"I'm very well. Thank you for your phone call today letting me know that the memorial for your dear mother has moved. The Met is such a fitting place to have it." Mrs. Foster continued, "She was a fine woman and you are so like her. You must be proud of her accomplishments, Laurel. I'm sure there are big things in your future, as well."

Laurel's stomach knotted and her palms got all clammy. She turned away and murmured a halfhearted agreement.

"Let me introduce Mac Hayes to you, Mrs. Foster. Mac, Mrs. Foster is a patron of the Met. She served on the board years ago."

Mac soothed his hand down Laurel's back at the same time he offered his hand to the elderly lady. "My pleasure."

"I'm sure, you young kids are off to a show, so I won't keep you. I'll see you at the auction, dear."

Laurel stood there for a moment watching the old woman walk down the street to meet up with a younger woman and a small child.

"Laurel? Are you all right?"

"I'm fine."

"You don't seem fine."

"I am. Drop it, Mac." That stupid reaction every time she met someone who knew her mother. It had to be related to the fact that it was coming up on a year since she'd died. She was missing her mother and being reminded of all that she had done in her life only made Laurel miss her more.

He slung his arm around her shoulders. "Okay, slugger. What do you feel like eating?"

They decided on an upscale Italian restaurant across the street from the pier. For an appetizer, Mac ordered stuffed mushroom caps. He took a drink of the Long Island iced tea he'd ordered and glanced at her. "Tell me about your bedroom furniture."

"What about it?" She sucked the stuffing out of the mushroom and then ate the tender vegetable.

"It's the only room in the house that's decorated like that."

She swirled her swizzle stick in the creamy Toasted Almond, a wonderful concoction of cream, amaretto, and khalua. Picking up the last mushroom, she held it to his mouth. His warm lips sucked the morsel from her fingers. Her stomach clenched at the moist feel of his tongue against her sensitive fingers. "I like that type of furniture. It knocks the tenets of architecture on its ear and reinforces functionalism to the tenth degree."

Mac wiped his mouth on a napkin. They'd pretty much finished the appetizer, and a man came by and cleared their dishes. It wasn't long afterward that the salad and then dinner arrived. "Functionalism?"

Mac dived into his spaghetti and meatballs, while Laurel speared her ziti dish. After chewing her bite, she said, "Functionalism came about in the late nineteenth and twentieth centuries that stripped architecture of all ornamentation so that a building's structure plainly expressed its function or purpose."

"Like Jacques-Emile Rhulmann. Art deco?"

"Yes," Laurel said incredulously, "You've grasped my meaning exactly and I'm thoroughly impressed."

"You might want to stop there before I have to point out one of your flaws."

Laurel closed her mouth, realizing that she'd almost insulted his intelligence again.

"That's all interesting, but I didn't ask you if you liked that type of furniture. I assumed that since your bedroom is decorated with it. I want to know why it's different from the rest of the house."

She waited while the young woman cleared their dishes, and Mac took the liberty of ordering tiramisu in the round for them to share—clouds of light mascarpone cream on a coffee-and-rum-soaked sponge cake, sprinkled with imported cocoa.

Once the waitress had moved on to fill their dessert order, Laurel said, "You're coming dangerously close to asking me to reveal my secret, Mac."

A muscle in his jaw flexed, and his expression turned adamant. "Your secret would be safe with me."

The rough, edgy sound in his voice thrilled her. "That's what I'm afraid of."

"There's nothing to fear from me. No pressure, no ties. He took her hand in his and absently rubbed his thumb against her palm. "No expectations. Easy."

Without even thinking about her answer, she said, "That's just what I'm looking for. Easy."

She tried to wrap her mind around Mac, but maybe she was thinking too much, and just as he said, she was grouping him into a category of guys instead of letting him be a three-dimensional man. True, he was a mechanic in his brother's dealership, yet he'd taken her to the premier theater district and frequented the area often. But how could that be? Black leather and musical theatre didn't seem to mesh.

This dinner had to be costing him a pretty penny, but he ordered without worry and even much of a perusal of the menu. More like a cosmopolitan guy.

"So you like art deco stuff. Like your mother?"

Laurel shifted. "Yes. My house was covered in art deco when I was a child. She'd collected for years before she actually thought about donating all of it to the museum."

"The chair and the table that I pulled out of your SUV were also what you'd call art deco, too."

"Yes."

Their tiramisu was delivered, the bites tasty and delicious. When the waitress came with the check, Mac pulled out a credit card to pay.

They left the restaurant and walked down the street toward his bike. "What now?" she asked. She didn't want to assume that he would spend the night with her, but she hoped.

"With a decadent meal like that, there's only one other thing to do."

"What's that?"

His dark mesmerizing gaze captivated her. "More decadence, of course."

Desire began a slow burn inside her, and a hopeful grin spread across her face. "I've always been fond of the word *debauchery*."

"Is that a fact?"

8

Your choice of aphrodisiac would be:

a. chocolate
b. oysters
c. champagne and strawberries
d. apple pie
 —*Excerpt from* Who's Your Hottie? *quiz,*
                              SPICE *magazine*

THAT'S WHAT LAUREL liked so much about Mac—his unpredictability. When it came to Mac, it was so easy to understand why she found him so tempting, so absolutely charming. He didn't take her home. Instead, he drove them back to his apartment.

No matter where Mac took her, Laurel knew how the night was going to end—with a deliciously forbidden fantasy fulfilled, and her completely sated. The man didn't do anything halfway, including giving as much sexual pleasure as he received.

The vibrating rumble of the motorcycle's engine between her thighs electrified her, building her anticipation for what was to come. Finally, the bike slowed. He used a key card to get into the lower-level parking garage. He parked in his space and cut the engine.

In one smooth, fluid motion he moved off the bike, then held out his hand to help her do the same, though her legs weren't quite as steady as his. Their helmets came off, and he stowed them in a small locker.

He took her hand and headed for the elevator. When the doors closed, sealing them in the quiet, private place, she stared up into his hot, hungry eyes and shivered.

When they reached his floor, they stepped out into the hall. As he turned to open the door, the light from a dim bulb in the hall illuminated his dark hair, haloing his head. He looked like a fallen angel, a dangerous outlaw, a man who lived on the edge.

She shouldn't be nervous; she knew exactly what she wanted to do. As they entered the apartment, there was a small light in the living room to illuminate their way and she took his hand and drew him toward the bedroom.

Once in the bedroom there was plenty of light from the streetlamps to show her the path to the bathroom. She pulled two candles out of her purse and set them down onto the bedside table. With a flick of a lighter, she lit both. The scent of vanilla and jasmine perfumed the air. With deliberate slowness, Laurel took off the leather jacket and set it on a chair by the window. In the dim light of the moon, she reached up to the first button on her shirt, and released the buttons and let it fall off her shoulders. Mac was just standing there, intensity and desire radiating off him like heat from the sun. "You, too," she coaxed softly. "I want to watch you undress, Mac."

Without any other prompting, he pulled his sweater

over his head, along with the T-shirt he was wearing underneath. When his hands went to the fastening of his jeans, Laurel reached for her jean snap as well. Their eyes met in the dimness, their chests heaving with anticipation. His eyes mirrored her own—deep, dark and shameless with an unrestrained quality that was spine-tingling.

When she was naked, she walked back to the bed and pulled a kitchen timer out of her purse. He looked at her with a puzzled frown, and she smiled. "That's for later."

Picking up one of the candles, she took his hand and led him into the bathroom. She set the candle on the sink and stepped into the tub. Reaching her hand out she whispered, "Come here."

Wordlessly he stepped inside and she sat down. "Sit down and lean your shoulders against my knees, drop your head back." He did so.

She turned on the water and adjusted the tap. Gently she ran her hands through his hair, wetting it, enjoying the sensation of the soft strands through her fingers.

"You're going to wash my hair?"

"Yes, do you mind?"

"Are you kidding?" He arched his back with a sigh and closed his eyes.

Shampoo lather dripped off his head, onto her bare thighs, pooling at her feet like clotted cream. In a sensual daze, she reveled in massaging his scalp, sending her hands through his hair as the humidity climbed in the room.

With his head flung back, the strong column of his throat was irresistible.

She leaned in and kissed him, running her mouth over the taut cords. She felt them vibrate with his soft moan. She moved up to his strong jawline, hovered over his mouth, kissing each corner.

She rinsed the lather out of his hair. Mac opened his eyes, questioning.

She smiled boldly and squeezed conditioner onto her palm.

"That smells good."

"You have the kind of hair that's not easy to tame."

"It's always been wild, ever since I was a kid."

"I heard about wild, but I think chick magnet was mentioned along with impulse control problems."

"I don't know about the chick magnet thing, but I have impulse control problems around you, Laurel."

She cupped his rough cheeks caressing his skin with her thumbs. "And you try to act so very cool."

"Aren't I?" She got lost in Mac's eyes. The pupils were dilated wells of infinite black bordered with pure summer-sky blue.

"Yes, you are. Very cool, very wonderful. Sweet and dangerous at the same time."

"Sweet?"

"Yes or have you forgotten about that little trip to the Met?"

"Okay, you got me."

"See. Sweet."

He smiled. The air was suddenly too thick and hot to breathe. This had to have been the most perfect day of her life. Letting out a shaky breath, she swallowed against the frantic flutter in her throat, her insides feeling like jelly. And it was all about Mac. Not his body or the way he looked, but him. Looking deeply into the bright pools she suddenly felt as if she'd been set free.

"Laurel," he said softly, then brought her aching mouth down to his. The kiss was hot and deep. She opened to him, her mouth moving against his with an urgent hunger that plunged to the heart of her. More than skin deep.

Gently she pulled away as if she was trying to resist the pull of a vortex. Through the misty haze eddying in the shower, his slumberous eyes captured hers, his dark, freshly washed hair slicked away from his striking face. "You're distracting me, Mr. Hayes."

"Is that good?"

"I haven't even gotten through the rest of my seduction."

"What's next?"

"Let's take a shower."

They rose and Laurel adjusted the faucet until the temperature was perfect.

"A shower by candlelight?"

"Oh, yes," she breathed. "We have to go by touch alone."

"Nice."

She couldn't stop herself from touching his slick, wet skin. Trailing her fingers up his muscular arms, deliberately taking the time to trace the barbed wire around his biceps and hesitated when it rubbed off.

"Mac, your tattoo is fading."

"What? Oh damn."

"It's not supposed to do that, is it?"

"No, but...it's not a real tattoo." He paused and she wished she could see his face. "I'm afraid of needles," he said sheepishly.

"Ah, okay. So, what is this?"

"Henna."

"Some bad boy you are." She giggled before continuing along his broad shoulders and down his muscled chest, which sent her deeper into that sensual trance. He felt deliciously warm and sleek, exceptionally hard in all the right places, and she savored his virile strength even as he brushed his hands across her pliant body so gently, so eloquently.

She reached for the soap and massaged him with slow, languorous strokes as she lathered along his belly, just grazing the top of his erection, up over the strong, sleek muscles of his chest, neck and shoulders.

He groaned softly, moving close enough to press his cock against her. She felt breathless, every one of her feminine nerve endings humming with tense awareness.

She turned him around and let the hot spray rinse the suds from the front of his body, while she soaped his back. He braced his hands against the tiled wall for support, bringing his heavy back muscles into taut relief as she applied skillful pressure to the firm tendons running along his spine.

With her hands on his waist, she turned his back to the shower for another quick rinse.

"My turn," he whispered, taking up the soap and lathering his hands. He turned her around and started working a silken magic down the muscles bisecting her spine, his firm touch spreading goose bumps along her flesh.

She closed her eyes, shivering as his palms slid over her hips and his big hands curved over her buttocks, squeezing and kneading her bottom. "That feels so good," she murmured.

He easily nudged her feet apart and slipped his fingers along the crevice between her legs, grazing the swollen lips of her sex before retreating again. She swallowed a moan at that teasing caress.

He readjusted the showerhead so the water poured along her back in a fall of sensual heat, and he chased the soapy suds down her spine with his palms, leaving her skin satiny-soft and clean from head to toe.

She gasped as his parted lips skimmed the side of her throat and his tongue licked the moisture beading on her skin. His breath was hot, and her nipples puckered, tingled, aching to be caressed by his hands, his mouth. Again.

A muscled arm slid around her waist, and he pulled her bottom to his groin so that his erection nestled cozily between her thighs. His free hand played with her breasts and lightly pinched her nipples, causing her to suck in a sharp breath and wriggle against him. His fingers strummed over her stomach, slid through her slick folds, opening her so that rivulets of water teased her clitoris, and his shaft glided along her tender, swollen flesh from behind.

Her entire body pulsed and ached, but she grabbed his hand to stop his alluring assault.

"No, not here."

He gently turned her around to face him, and the water cascaded over her shoulders and down her curves. She experienced a moment of vulnerability that had nothing to do with her naked body. Physically, she was all his in every way, but it was the raw emotions working their way up to the surface that made her feel so exposed to him. And as a man so in tune to her, he seemed to sense that change.

"Are you okay?" he asked, brushing a wet strand of hair off her cheek with his fingers.

The warmth and compassion in his touch lingered, wrapping intimately around her heart, urging her to divulge her personal thoughts. "I just didn't expect this...to feel so marvelous."

The genuine caring reflected in his striking gaze clutched at her heart. "Me, either. Guess we're not good at one-night stands," he said simply and with understanding.

"When it comes to you, Mac, no." Her voice trembled, another show of emotion that slipped past her barriers.

He stared at her for a long moment, then cradled the back of her head in his hand and brought her mouth to his for a slow, soft kiss, as if that physical contact was the best way he knew how to comfort her.

His method worked because he made her forget everything but the glorious, desirable way he made her feel. She opened to him, clung to him, and when his warm, damp tongue slid into her mouth, she greedily accepted it.

Her heart beat so erratically beneath her breast, she was certain he'd be able to feel the wild tempo against his chest. Thick hot steam built around them, and the moisture from the shower made their skin slippery, erotically so. His breathing roughened, and the kiss deepened, grew more urgent and evocative. He backed her up against the warm tiled wall, ruthlessly pinning her there with his hard muscled body. His palms slid slowly down her sides, and he grasped her bottom in his hands and ground his hips against hers, his solid, unmistakable erection causing a wet, silken friction along the lips of her sex.

She shuddered and held on to his shoulders, her need for him becoming a tangible thing, strong and power-ful and nearly overwhelming in its intensity. She wrenched her mouth from his, panting. "Time to go to the bed."

"Right, the seduction. Sorry, I keep losing track every time I touch you."

"I'll make it worth your while."

They got out and toweled off. Holding hands they walked back to the bedroom. "Lay down on your back," Laurel requested as she picked up the timer. "This is the deal. We're going to have the Big O Marathon. That's twenty-six point four minutes of oral stimulation."

She set the kitchen timer and without saying another word, she straddled his body and thrust her sex against his mouth. All thoughts fled. All that remained was the liquid, swirling sensation of his lips and his strong, eager tongue lapping and laving her, flicking expertly across her most sensitive flesh. She gripped damp, silky hand-fuls of his hair and pushed herself against his mouth. His growl of satisfaction reverberated through her body.

She rolled her hips back and forth and softly whis-pered, "Oh, yes...oh that's so good."

Just when she was beginning to feel the tense spiral, she pulled away from him and turned around. Pressing her chest and arms against the bed, she raised her bot-tom into the air, demanding, "Suck me. Lick me." She taunted him with her body and her desire. She abandoned herself to the shifting energy between them. He grabbed her hips tightly, dragging her wet mound toward his hot mouth. She cried out at the moist contact.

He found her pulsing clit, and his tongue circled it with wet flicks and slow, suctioning swirls, accelerating her heart rate off the charts. Then his lips closed over her, and he took her eagerly, hotly, greedily, sending her over the razor-sharp edge of orgasm just as the timer went off.

It took her a moment to catch her breath and when she could, she said, "You know exactly what to do to make me come."

She rose and turned to face him, his eyes dark pools of pulsing, heaving desire.

She smiled and picked up the timer.

He closed his eyes and said hoarsely, "I'll *never* last that long."

"We'll see," she said huskily, moving over him. He was hard and hot as she slid her hand around him, fisting his cock snugly. She moved her hand up and down, and with her other, she used a fingertip to swirl it around his hot, smooth flesh. He cried out and arched off the bed.

She played with him, discovering his body with her hands and her lips. He squeezed his eyes shut and shuddered violently when she took him into her mouth.

She loved his warm, salty taste, his musky male smell. His erection pulsed between her hands, against her caressing tongue.

He gripped fistfuls of her hair. His tone grew more pleading as she experimented with her tongue, with her hands. The bolder she was, the harder he thrashed. She pulled him deeper, swallowing him whole, sucking him hard, circling with her tongue, milking him with her hands.

His hands tightened in her hair. "Laurel, damn." He convulsed and exploded.

And she had minutes to spare.

MAC SAT at the kitchen table with the Monday morning *Wall Street Journal* open in front of him, but the articles and daily information about the stock market couldn't hold his interest on this day.

He was thinking about Laurel sleeping so soundly in his brother's bed, in his brother's apartment. And how all this was such a sham. Last night, she'd teased saying he wasn't much of a bad boy with his henna tattoo and she was right.

But damn the way they had connected made him feel like his heart was going to burst. It had been hard to leave her silky body, but he couldn't sleep with his conscious bothering him. He knew he had to tell her who he was. The charade had gone on too long.

He'd started this affair with open eyes. His goal had been to get to know her, let her know him. But she didn't really know the real him. And as time passed, he was getting in deeper. He already had so much at stake. She'd allowed him into her life, into her home and all on false pretenses.

He'd broken the cardinal bad-boy rule that he stay in charge. Stay indifferent. However, when it came to Laurel, he couldn't be, either. He wanted her in his life beyond the brief affair she wanted.

"That better be coffee I smell or I'm going to hurt someone."

Mac turned at the sound of Laurel's sleep-husky voice, and his body stirred at the sexy way she filled out his shirt, along with the adorable blush on her cheeks. Oh, yeah, he could get used to having her at his place on a regular basis.

"Fresh pot," he said, smiling. "Want some?"

"I want very much." She came up to the counter beside him and pushed her fingers through her softly disheveled hair, appearing self-conscious and wary. "What time is it?"

"About six-thirty, still plenty of time to get you home and to work.

Grabbing a chipped mug from Tyler's cupboard, he poured the steaming coffee to the rim.

It seemed so natural and easy to slip his arm around her waist, lower his mouth to hers and kiss her with heat and passion that seemed to grow stronger every time he touched her. Her hands came to rest on his chest, her small palms warm and comforting against his naked skin. He didn't know that he needed this touch until he heard her sigh against his mouth, a surrender to the feelings that were swamping him, too. She pressed into him and he could feel her lush unfettered breasts, flatten against his chest.

Before he gave in to the urge to find out what, if anything at all, she was wearing beneath his shirt, he pulled back and skimmed his thumb along her damp lower lip. He exhaled heavily and said, "There's something I want to tell you."

He hesitated realizing that he was being a coward, but once those words left his lips, he would have no control over her actions. He was more worried about hurting her. His heart hammering in his chest, he ran his hands through his hair.

She moved smoothly out of his embrace, seemingly a bit skittish. Was she somehow sensing his unease? She walked over to the table and spooned sugar into her coffee. Suddenly, she stopped stirring and reached down to finger the *Wall Street Journal* and slanted him a speculative look.

"You read the *Journal?*"

"For the articles," he joked, but Laurel didn't laugh or smile.

"I thought only stockbroker types and financial wizards read this."

It was a perfect opening for him to tell her who he was. He opened his mouth to speak.

"I could never see myself with a stockbroker." She took a sip of her coffee, unaware of the blow she'd just delivered. "So damned uptight, worried about appearances and money. It all seems too cold and calculating to me. Just like all the men and women at my father's firm. That's why I vowed never to date anyone who works there."

His throat tight and a hole where his heart should be, he clamped his mouth shut around the words he almost spilled forth.

He still had an opportunity to show her that he wasn't anything like that. If he kept his mouth shut it would give him a little more time. It was starting to feel like borrowed time.

"I'm sorry." She turned toward him. "What were you going to say?"

Slowly he reached into his back pocket and pulled

out the Nine Inch Nails concert tickets that his brother
had dropped off this morning.

She stared at them transfixed, looking totally winded.
As if she'd finally come back to life, she turned and set
the mug down with enough force to nearly crack it in
half. Then she closed her eyes and braced both hands on
the countertop, and he saw her chest rise, as if she
couldn't catch her breath. It wasn't the response he expected—he'd expected her to squeal and jump up and
down. But this response was even better—he liked it a
lot.

Finally getting some air into her lungs, she turned
and looked at him, narrowing her eyelids. "Damn you,
Hayes," she breathed; then she caught him by the hair,
pulled his head down and gave him a kiss that about
blew his jeans to smithereens.

Laughing against her mouth, his whole body going
on full alert, he slid his arms around her hips. "Tell me
something else you like so that I can run right out and
buy it for you."

"How did you get these?"

"My brother has connections. He was a roadie before he opened the shop. He called in a favor for me."

She gave his hair another yank and deepened the
kiss, and Mac got real serious, real quick, and he
dragged her up against him. She made a low sound and
slid her arms around him neck, and suddenly Mac
couldn't breathe, either. Cupping the back of her head
gently in his hands, he fought for air, his heart hammering. He changed the angle of her head, then sealed his
mouth hungrily against hers. He would never get them
to the bedroom in time. Never.

Laurel moved against him, and he nearly groaned, a pulsating heat coursing through him. In desperation, he turned and set her on the counter, wedging his hips between her thighs. She hooked her legs around his waist and moved flush against him and he nearly lost his mind. This was a fantasy he hadn't even had yet.

9

Where would you prefer your hottie live?

a. suburbs
b. apartment
c. on the open road
d. village loft

—*Excerpt from* Who's Your Hottie? *quiz,*
SPICE *magazine*

LAUREL BARELY GOT to her office on time, thanks to that quick morning tryst in the kitchen. She'd had to hightail it home and then get dressed, but the memories of Mac's hard body were difficult to get out of her head.

She had to pass Mark Dalton's desk and he pointedly looked at his watch. Even after she'd reprimanded him last week, he hadn't changed his attitude and Laurel was getting heartily sick of it.

She wasn't going to let Mark ruin her wonderful weekend, except for that tense moment when Mac said he had something to tell her. She thought he was breaking up with her. The look on his face had been so serious and the thought of never seeing him again had made her throat tight. But then he'd pulled out those tickets. She'd been overwhelmed that he would remember her favorite band much less go to the lengths he had to get the tickets.

Settled behind her desk, she doodled on the pad next to her computer, dreamily remembering his clever hands and mouth.

Rain pelted against the wide windows on a dreary day, but Laurel felt anything but miserable. She felt as buoyed as if she was bobbing on a warm wonderful sea with nothing but beauty surrounding her.

A sharp rap on her door brought her head around. Mark Dalton lounged in the doorway. He had a sheaf of papers in his hand. She froze when she recognized them as the draft of her presentation for Coyle and Hamilton.

She jumped up from her chair. "What are you doing with those?"

"Your careless assistant must have left them in the copier. So, you're going after Coyle and Hamilton? Ambitious," he said in a tone that dripped with sarcasm and indicated she didn't have a prayer of succeeding.

Laurel came around her desk, matching his cold stare and snatched the papers out of Mark's hands. "Don't you have work to do, because if you don't I'd be happy to assign you something," she said between clenched teeth.

"Laurel, do you have a moment?"

Mr. Herman stood a few steps away, watching the exchange between them. It irked her that Mark didn't seem to care as he snickered and walked away.

"Yes," she replied, meeting his somber gaze with one full of challenge. She wouldn't back down like she'd been taught. She couldn't act like her mother wanted her to. She was sick of being treated as if she didn't have a place here or was suddenly incompetent.

"Mark told me this morning that you are working on a presentation for Coyle and Hamilton."

The slimy tattletale. "That's true. I have a meeting the beginning of next week."

"I think it might be a good idea to allow Mark to work on it with you or let him take over."

Instead of retreating into herself, anger surged inside her, but she held it rigidly in check. She would not act unprofessional, but she was through with being pushed around. "What? On what grounds?"

"Laurel, we both know that Mark has more experience than you do. You should take advantage of his expertise."

"That may be true, but I've brought plenty of clients into this business and I resent being told to my face that I'm incompetent. I'm keeping the Coyle and Hamilton account. I'll land it, too," she said firmly.

"You're getting very close to insubordination, Laurel," he warned.

"That's interesting, Mr. Herman, because you stood right there while Mark was insubordinate to me. In fact, you've done nothing about his attitude. If anything, you've encouraged it."

He narrowed his eyes. "I'm urging you to rethink the Coyle and Hamilton deal, Laurel."

"No. I deserve the chance to follow through. I made the initial contact and my presentation is very sound."

"Let me see it," he said impatiently.

Reluctantly she handed him the draft. He took his time going through each slide and when he was finished, he sighed and raised his eyes to meet hers. He looked like a man about to eat some crow. "Where did you get this unitedthinking concept?"

"I came up with it myself."

"It's very good, Laurel. Brilliant, in fact. It takes all the aspects of our company and puts them into a simple, powerful model. I'd like to take this to Waterford and Scott. With your permission, of course."

"That's fine. I have your blessing to go forward?" she asked.

"Yes. Keep me posted."

He went to turn away, but Laurel said, "Mr. Herman?"

He stopped and turned back to face her. "Yes, Laurel?"

"If Mark had more seniority than me, why did you promote me?"

He shook his head. "You weren't my choice, Laurel."

"What do you mean?"

He rubbed his temples. "I was overruled."

"By whom?"

"Mr. Scott," he said and closed her door on his way out.

Laurel stood there for a moment trying to absorb the bombshell Mr. Herman had just dropped. Mr. Scott? The Mr. Scott who owned half of the company? He didn't know her name. Did he? How could that be? How could he have insisted that she be promoted over someone who had six years experience over her? It didn't make sense to her.

Before she had a chance to think about it anymore, her phone rang and Laurel picked it up.

"How's my favorite sister-in-law?"

"I'm your only sister-in-law," Laurel said sinking into her chair, focusing on Haley's voice to keep her mind off Mr. Scott.

Haley chuckled and said, "That's why you're my favorite. How goes it with that gorgeous biker?"

"It has its ups and downs, but he was sweet enough to get tickets to a sold out Nine Inch Nails concert at the Garden."

"What night?"

"Wednesday."

"Good. You do remember that the *SPICE* party is on Friday?"

"Damn, it's a good thing you called. I totally forgot about it. I've been so busy."

"I'd stay busy with a man like that. He was *sweet* enough to buy you concert tickets? Doesn't sound like any bad boy I've ever known."

"I know. He doesn't always act the way I expect him to. The inconsistency in his character is weird."

"As long as he treats you with respect, does it really matter?"

"No. It doesn't. It's just that I like him a lot. I'm sure he's also not into alternative rock music, either. His taste goes more toward rock classics like Bruce Springsteen and the Beatles."

"I never did get that alternative rock stuff, either. What are you going to wear?"

"That black lace mini I bought the last time I went shopping and a bright pink top."

"Purchases which surprised the hell out of me. Dylan's always telling me how conservative you are with your Donna Karan suits and button-down clothing. Is this guy having some kind of an influence on you?"

"He's teaching me about being a rebel. A role I have to say I kind of like. I actually have on a red blouse beneath my conservative gray suit today."

"Do you? I bet it's buttoned all the way to your throat."

"No. As a matter of fact, it has a V-neck, thank you very much. So what are you doing?"

"Kicking some ideas around for the June issue of *SPICE*. I've got an article on how to bag a groomsman, wedding night sex ideas, and what's new and hot in rings."

"You live such an interesting life."

"Do I hear a note of dissatisfaction in your voice? Is this about your job?"

"Accounting also has its ups and downs. When I try to make a difference, I get treated like I'm incompetent. But I think I made an impression this morning with a proposal to a new client."

"Have you ever thought about doing something else?"

"It wouldn't make sense to leave a job I've spent years building."

"Laurel, everyone has dreams. I know you do. Dreams are the most precious, priceless things in the world. I went after mine and got Dylan in the process. It was a win-win situation. You should think about it. Change and risk are uncomfortable but the rewards are worth it. Of course, not everyone is a risk taker. I'll talk to you later."

After Laurel hung up the phone, she felt stung by Haley's comment. Risk taker. Mac had said that, too. She wasn't naturally a risk taker, but giving up everything that she'd worked for wasn't easy, either.

Her thoughts drifted back to that 27th Street store and the empty windows. She could envision them filled with her designs just waiting to be bought and used.

Haley had said that dreams were precious. She was

right, but did Laurel have what it took to take such an illusive idea and make it reality?

The more she thought about this, the more tangible it seemed. Opening up her own business, being her own boss and doing what she loved. What could be wrong with that? She could call it Fun and Funktion Furniture. The upside was that she would get to do exactly what she wanted, but the downside was the real possibility she could lose a large chuck of income and look foolish. She was very fond of her security. So she wasn't a risk taker. She was cautious, that's all.

Wait a minute. She wasn't all that cautious. She had stood up to Mark and Mr. Herman and found out an intriguing fact. She'd have to make time to talk to Mr. Scott as soon as she could. That would require a risk— she wasn't quite sure she wanted to know why Mr. Scott insisted she be promoted.

In spite of a pair of leather pants and a racy black mini hanging in her closet, she was still a far cry from taking that big a risk.

Small changes. Perhaps Mac had influenced her to take a few more chances, but this was all temporary. Once he was out of her life, she'd fall back into her safe and sure ways.

Great, just great.

THE GARDEN BUZZED with energy as Mac and Laurel entered through the glass doors Wednesday night. They had great seats up front and started making their way down. Laurel had been to the Garden plenty of times and the old familiar arena was bustling with activity. People milling in through the numerous doorways, stagehands working on the lights and microphones on the stage at the west end of the building.

This was actually the fourth Madison Square Garden, settled atop Union station—the same Madison Square Garden where Frank Sinatra, Elton John, and even Elvis had played. It gave her goose bumps to be in a building so steeped in entertainment history.

About halfway down the stairs, Laurel passed a very pregnant woman, but Mac stopped and offered her his hand. "Can I help you to your seat?"

Laurel watched dumbfounded as he assisted the woman to where she needed to go.

When they got to their seats, Laurel sat down and turned to Mac. "I really don't know who you are."

There was momentary panic in his eyes that made her stomach twist. For the first time, she wondered if he was hiding something, but his eyes cleared and she thought maybe it was only her imagination.

"I'm just a guy."

"I don't think so. If you were just a guy, I wouldn't be so attracted to you."

A slow, cautious smile curved his mouth. "Why not?" He lifted her hand to his lips and kissed it.

A smile lifted the corner of her mouth. "*Just guys* don't attract a lot of women because they rarely care what we want, have an attitude, and piss women off."

"Have you ever considered that it's not my charm that keep us together, but you? That you are the exciting one, the fun one, and interesting?"

Skepticism filled her voice. "Don't try to butter me up or change the conversation. I can't quite figure you out."

"Do you need to figure me out? Why can't you just enjoy being with me?"

A popcorn vender came by and Mac raised his hand. She waited while he paid for the two bags of popcorn before she spoke. "I do enjoy being with you. You've taught me a lot."

"About what?"

"It's healthy to have fun once in a while. Don't take myself too seriously."

"How many days have you taken off in the last year?"

"None, well, except for a dentist appointment."

Leaning back, he popped a kernel in his mouth.

"My sister-in-law Haley says I'm not a risk taker."

"Do you want to be a risk taker, Laurel?"

"She said that not everyone takes risks. She may be right. I like feeling secure."

"There's nothing wrong with that, Laurel."

"No, I guess not, but I think about it a lot."

"You did take a risk on me. You approached me and gave me your number."

Laurel felt gratitude toward Mac for pointing that information out to her. "You're right. I did."

Mac looked into Laurel's eyes and his heart lurched in his chest. She was so unique and he couldn't regret pretending to be a bad boy to get her attention. He'd had such great fun with her. He wanted her in his life.

"You also contacted Coyle and Hamilton. How is that going, by the way?" Mac asked, interested in her progress.

"I've completed the presentation, but something odd happened on Monday that I didn't get a chance to tell you."

"What's that?"

"Mr. Herman said that he didn't recommend me for the promotion."

"Isn't he your supervisor?"

"Yes, but he said it was Mr. Scott who overruled him when Mr. Herman recommended Mark Dalton."

"Did you talk to Mr. Scott?" Mac asked.

"I tried to make an appointment yesterday, but he's out of town until Monday."

"When is your presentation?"

"On Tuesday morning," Laurel replied.

He had to make sure they didn't end up in that building at the same time. This juggling act needed to end soon, but Mac decided he'd do it after the auction and her presentation. He'd tell her Tuesday night for sure after everything had settled down.

How she took the news was important to him. Their short time together was no longer just about great sex and how compatible they were in bed. Yes, she was his perfect match sexually; open for anything that gave them pleasure, just like last night's erotic fantasy. But it was becoming increasingly obvious to him, with each passing day, being her temporary lover wasn't going to do it for him. He wanted—needed—more than a short-term affair.

"So tell me something about this band."

"You've really never heard of Nine Inch Nails?"

"Nope. I told you, I'm a classics guy."

"Trent Reznor is the lead singer and he writes all their music. The band started in 1989 and revitalized the Goth scene."

"You were a Goth queen? In 1989 you were only eleven."

"I was never a Goth queen, more like a closet Goth."

"But you did it on the sly at your girlfriend's house."

"Yes," Laurel giggled. "I did."

"So Trent is big in the alternative music scene?"

"He's as big as David Bowie."

The stadium was filled to capacity and the lights dimmed as the warm-up band raced onto the stage. They played for forty-five minutes until Nine Inch Nails came on stage.

Blasting a loud rendition of something that sounded like "Closer" through their high-amp sound system, the throbbing music had a good beat to it, but it couldn't compare to the hard-rocking lyrics of Springsteen. Mac shook his head with a small twist of amusement. He would never have pegged Laurel for an alternative rock fan. Just another interesting tidbit that made up Laurel Malone.

He could spend the rest of his life discovering all her alluring facets and never tire of finding each gem.

"I KNOW A GREAT CAFÉ that serves warm apple pie à la mode," Laurel said as they came out of the Garden. "But we'll have to take a cab instead of the subway. It's quite a walk from the nearest station and not exactly in the best part of town."

The Garden was clearing rapidly and Laurel's ears throbbed from the ear-splitting music.

"Sounds good," Mac replied.

When they hit the street they waved down a cabbie and were soon deposited in front of Molly's Café.

The café had changed very little since Laurel had been there last. The same row of chrome-trimmed stools along the front counter, the same plate-glass showcase by the front door, the same high-back booths along the windows. The only thing that had changed was the décor. The gaudy geometric-patterned curtains had been replaced with vertical blinds. And the stools and seats in the booths were now upholstered in a subdued tan instead of the bright orange that Laurel remembered. Too bad. She liked the retro look of the place before it had been upgraded.

A waitress came over to their table and they each ordered apple pie à la mode with coffee.

"How did you know about this place?"

"Dylan and I used to come here a lot when we were in college."

"Your brother?"

The waitress was back with their pie and poured them each a cup of coffee.

"Right. He's married to the editor of *SPICE* magazine, Haley Lawton."

"*SPICE*, that racy women's magazine."

"Hey, it has great articles."

"Sure," he said, chuckling. "*How To Make Him Beg In Bed* and *Looking For Mr. Right*. I bet."

She laughed. "I didn't know you read *SPICE*, although some of your moves in bed are very spice-worthy."

"If you got your moves from *SPICE*, I'd say keep reading it."

"I will because I love it. Speaking of *SPICE*. Are you still going to the party with me?"

"That's this Friday?"

"Yes. Haley's counting on us to be there." The next

words came out in a rush. "Next Tuesday night is the auction, the anniversary of my mother's death. Do you think you could escort me?"

Mac shifted and looked away. When she was about to withdraw her invitation, sure he was uncomfortable, he responded.

"Do I have to wear a tux?"

"Is that okay?"

"Sure, I have one...uh...I can borrow."

"Great. It's settled." She took a bite of her pie. "The place may have changed, but the pie is still scrumptious." In a hesitant voice, she asked. "So Ted is your half brother?"

"We have the same mother and different fathers."

"Are you close to your father?" She saw him hesitate and he clenched his jaw tight. She realized that he may not be interested in telling her anything about his past. "I'm sorry. I didn't mean to pry."

His expression of disquiet remained for a moment, then he gave a noncommittal shrug. "You know how it is between fathers and sons."

Laurel nodded. "Your brother Ted is sure doing well for himself. My father only hires the very best people. My friend Sherry really likes working for him. She says he's funny and very fair."

He met her eyes, a strange feeling unfolding in her stomach when she saw how solemnly he was watching her. He stared at her for a moment; then he glanced down, as if he saw something that disturbed him. Folding a paper napkin by his cup, he hesitated for a moment, then finally spoke. "Ted's a good guy," was all he said.

No talking about family. She couldn't blame him. She wasn't too keen on talking about hers.

"So, how long have you been working for Tyler?"

"Ever since he opened the place."

"Have you ever thought about doing anything else?"

"What do you mean?"

"Go to college?"

"Why not just fix motorcycles?"

"Why not do more?" she countered. "You really know a lot about art deco and the Met. Ever thought about art?"

They stared at each other for a moment, not speaking, not looking away.

"No, I never did. I do love the Met, but never thought of it as a career."

"I'm just wondering if there's a hope or dream you'd ever considered pursuing."

"I like my job." He studied her for a moment and she looked out the window watching the occasional late-night cab whiz by. "Have you?" he asked, speculation thick in his eyes.

"Maybe."

Feeling as though she had something heavy inside her chest, she forced herself to meet his gaze. Mac was watching her with a steely look in his eyes. "What are you getting at Laurel?"

Releasing a heavy sigh, she shook her head. "I feel very close to you, Mac. I want to show you something that is very important to me." She hesitated a minute, picking at an imperfection on her mug, then looked out the window again. "This weekend. It'll involve an over-night stay out of town. Are you busy?"

"No."

"What about your job?"

"I can get the time off if you want me to."

"I want you to."

Mac's gaze never wavered from hers and there was a softness in his eyes that did something warm and wonderful to her heart. He sat forward and took her hand in his, his warm fingers stroking her palm. She experienced a twist of apprehension, suspecting that he was going to push her to reveal where she wanted him to go and what she wanted him to see. And she didn't want to explain it to him. She wanted him to see it.

There was a drawn-out silence; then he glanced up at her, his gaze intent. "What time do you want to leave?"

She smiled and squeezed his hand. "First thing Saturday morning if you don't mind."

"Nope."

"Want to take the bike?"

"I would love to, but it would be better if we took my SUV."

"All right. So I guess the question is, do you want to go to your place or mine?"

"To sleep?"

"Ah, I think we're going to do more than sleep."

She returned his infectious grin. The softness in his eyes intensified, causing a strong, rippling ache through her heart.

They left the diner and headed for his place to pick up his clothes, then it was on to her brownstone.

MAC HAD KNOWN that pushing her at the diner would be the wrong thing to do. She intended to show him something very special and a peculiar feeling filled up his chest. When they crossed the threshold of her room and got to the bed, she grabbed the material of his shirt in her hands and pulled him close. Her mouth softly brushed his, the warmth and moistness of the kiss making his pulse erratic. She licked his bottom lip slowly— very slowly.

Opening his mouth beneath hers, Mac deepened the kiss. She changed the angle of her head, perfecting the seal of her mouth against his; then she smoothed her hand down his chest, undoing the buttons of his shirt with little flicks of her thumb. Holding his head immobile with her other hand, she pulled his shirt out of the waistband of his jeans, then lightly dragged her thumbnail across his nipple. Mac jerked, her touch sending a sharp current of sensation through him when she lightly rolled the hardened nub under her fingers.

He wanted to grab her and drag her beneath him, but her seduction was too sweet, too arousing, to let go. With a wild flurry of excitement building in him, Mac tightened his muscles against her tormenting touch, yielding his mouth to hers as she prolonged the kiss. Just as she stroked the inside of his bottom lip with her tongue, she trailed her fingernail down the hard ridge of flesh beneath his fly, and the dual sensations nearly put Mac through the roof. His breathing turned heavy, and it took every ounce of control he had to remain still and unmoving beneath her lightly exploring hands and mouth. She stroked the full length of his hard, thick arousal again, and Mac sucked in a ragged breath, releasing a guttural sound against her mouth while she trailed her nails between his legs and down the sensitive base.

Working her mouth slowly against his, she shifted slightly, then used both hands to undo his belt. She pulled the belt free of the loops and dropped it on the floor, then slid her long fingers beneath his waistband. Her intimate touch electrified him, and he lifted his head and drew her tongue deeply into his mouth, the pulsating hardness in his groin nearly exploding as she carefully drew his zipper down. With the same slow care, she freed him, and Mac abruptly ceased to breathe. Unable to remain passive one second longer, he caught her and ground his mouth hungrily against hers, heat searing through him as she lightly smoothed her thumb over the moist slick tip of his arousal.

Grasping her face between his hands, Mac gazed at her, his breathing labored. Her eyes dark and heavy-lidded, her full, sensual mouth swollen from the urgency of his kiss, she was the temptress, the vixen, his ultimate fantasy. He stroked the line of her jaw with his thumbs, her pulse frantic beneath the heels of his hands. He wanted her naked on top of him, he wanted to be buried so deep inside her that he would become part of her, and he wanted to let go of the heat that had him hard and erect.

With quick and efficient movements, she removed her clothes and pushed him back onto the bed. He felt her take a deep, unsteady breath; then she kissed both his eyes closed. "Don't move," she whispered. She pulled free of his hold, and Mac clenched his teeth against the sharp sense of separation, the ache in him growing heavier. Resting one arm over his eyes, he tried not to think, not to feel. He was at the point where a single touch could set him off, and the thought of sinking deep inside her was enough to send him over the edge.

Mac sucked in a deep breath when she took his hard, pulsating flesh in her hand, stroking him with the lightest of touches. Her gaze locked with his, she stroked him again, and Mac's face contorted at the sharp, intense pleasure that ricocheted through him. Laurel cupped him in both hands, her pulse quickening, and Mac rose up on one elbow and pulled her toward him. She resisted. Moistening her lips, she held his gaze for an instant longer, then looked down. His heart hammering like a wild thing in his chest, Mac watched her as she put the condom in place, then slowly began to roll it down, her touch soft and unsteady. Mac thought his heart was going to come right through his chest as he watched her carefully sheath him, and he gritted his teeth, need and want and a fever of desire reaching a flash point. The instant she had the protection in place, he rolled, carrying her beneath him. Urgently finding her mouth with his, he drew up her knees and roughly settled himself in the cradle of her thighs. Emitting a low groan, he entered her, his awareness shattering, a sunburst of sensation. Then he slipped into a space where there was nothing except him and Laurel—and a driving urgency.

It took Mac a long time to calm down after the earthshaking climax. And it took him a long time before he could relax his hold on her. But finally he was able to collect enough strength to ease back a little. By then she was deeply asleep. He stirred enough to pull the covers over them. He closed his eyes and tightened his hold, a knot of raw emotion climbing up his throat.

He took a deep breath, but that persistent ache remained, right in the vicinity of his heart—a tenderness and yearning that seemed to grow with each encounter with Laurel. It was as if she gave a little part of herself to him each time they were together, each time they had sex.

Last night they'd definitely had hot, uninhibited sex. But now it felt like they'd made love in the purest sense. Stunned and shaken by the realization, and feeling overwhelmingly vulnerable, he struggled to contain the emotions rioting within him. Emotions he was helpless to deny.

He was playing with his future here. Laurel had become much too important to him to keep up his facade. But at this point, he felt he had to put off telling her until her life settled down a little.

The fear of losing her was almost as powerful as those unnamed emotions he refused to identify.

10

What form of flirty fun would you most like with your hottie?

a. wrap yourself in a flag and let him unravel you
b. play cops and robbers, so he'll frisk you
c. get a tattoo in a sexy place to show him later,
d. show him you know how to balance his spread-
   sheet.
   —*Excerpt from* Who's Your Hottie? *quiz,*
                              SPICE *magazine*

ON FRIDAY AT NOON, Laurel pushed open the doors to her father's suite of offices. Walking up to Sherry's desk, she smiled when her friend looked up.

"Hey there. Long time no see."

Laurel set the café mocha in front of Sherry, taking a seat on the cushy chair near her desk.

"For me? A bribe?" Sherry's gaze narrowed skeptically.

"A peace offering for being so distracted and not calling you." She did feel guilty. She wasn't one of those women who got a boyfriend and forgot about her friends.

"So what's going on?"

"Work, the auction and Mac."

"Mac? Oooh. Who's Mac?"

Promise you won't laugh.

"Would I do that?"

"Yes, you would."

"I did one of those *SPICE* quizzes. *Who's Your Hottie?*"

Sherry took a drink of the steaming liquid and sighed. Sherry turned her focus from the fragrant cup to Laurel's face. "I did that quiz, too. Who was yours?"

"Remember last week when we went to Hayes Cycles to get Michael a bike?"

"Sure. He loved it by the way."

"I sort of threw myself at the mechanic there."

"Don't tell me. Bad-boy biker."

"Mac is the owner's brother."

Sherry sent a quick look over her shoulder toward her boss's office, a speculative look on her face.

"What?"

"Nothing. I didn't know that Tyler and Mr. Tolliver had another brother who worked at Hayes Cycles."

"Guess so, anyway, he shows up at my brownstone and it's been a whirlwind ever since."

"Good for you. It's about time you had yourself some fun, Laurel. Some of the stiff necks you date are so boring."

"Stop it. You were lucky enough to find Michael. Some of us are not that lucky."

"What about this Mac guy? It could turn into something."

"No. He's really not someone that I can see for the

long term. One of those passionate burn out types of relationships."

"Those are fine as long as you don't engage your heart, Laurel."

"That's the trick, but there's no problem in that area."

"What are you doing tonight? Maybe you and Mac can meet us downtown for dancing?" Sherry suggested.

"I'm going to the *Who's Your Hottie? SPICE* Party at POSH tonight. Haley got the brilliant idea from me. She put the invite on the *SPICE* Web site and the first one hundred couples to respond get in."

"It's impossible to get into that club. Tough door. I once saw those beefy security guys evict some guy from line because he didn't have a couple of babes on each arm."

"Hey, why don't you and Michael come tonight? It'll be fun and you can meet Mac."

"I don't want to crash Haley's party."

"Haley won't care. I'll leave word at the door."

Sherry nodded. "So what are you doing here?"

"I came to see my father. I haven't been able to get him on the phone. I've left three messages and he hasn't returned my call. I wanted to talk to him about the auction. It's Monday night and I'm not sure he's even coming."

"Oh sure. He's coming. He wouldn't miss your mother's tribute."

"I don't know, Sherry. He's been so distant lately and he won't participate in anything to do with the auction."

"He's a busy person, Laurel. Maybe he's leaving the details up to you and Dylan."

"Maybe."

"It's too bad he's not here. He and Mr. Tolliver had a lunch meeting with a client."

"Oh, well, it was good to see you, Sherry."

So she had lied to her friend. A little. Mac was more than a bad-boy biker. He was quickly becoming a close confidant and she wasn't sure what she thought about that. Whether she wanted to get personal or not, it was happening. Except it didn't seem to be a two-way street. The more she spilled about herself, the deeper she felt herself sink.

Was sinking good?

Only if you didn't drown, Laurel thought.

MAC LOOKED OVER at Laurel as he drove his sleek sports car toward upscale Chelsea where POSH was near 26th Street, for the *SPICE* party. She looked pensive. "What's up?"

She turned toward him. "Nothing. I just haven't had a chance to get hold of my father to talk about the change of venue and him attending the auction on Tuesday."

"Did you leave him a message?"

"Yes. All the details."

"Maybe he doesn't think he needs to call back. Guys are like that."

That got him a small smile. "Yeah. I'm sure everything is fine."

The auction was going to be a major problem. Laurel's father would be attending which meant he would definitely recognize Mac. He was torn between being available to Laurel on a night that was sure to be emotional for her with the fact that he could so easily be exposed before he had the chance to tell her about who he really was.

He wasn't quite sure how he was going to handle it.

Moments later they pulled up to the club and a valet took care of Mac's car. When they reached the door, a burly man blocked their entrance.

"Private party tonight."

"Yes, my name should be on the list. Laurel Malone and Mac Hayes."

The man perused the clipboard in his hands. "Yes. Go right in."

"I wanted to make sure that you have Sherry Black and Michael Vega on the list."

Mac groaned inwardly suddenly feeling trapped. If Sherry saw him….

"Yes, they're on the list."

"Thanks," Laurel said as she brushed past the guard and preceded Mac into the club.

"Hi there," Haley yelled enthusiastically at them as they came through the door. She was clad in a silver-beaded dress and Laurel's darkly handsome brother was impeccably dressed in a black turtleneck and designer trousers.

Mac felt underdressed next to the stylishly dressed couple, but Laurel insisted that his usual clothing was what Haley wanted him to wear. Standing next to her brother brought home the fact that Mac preferred to dress like Dylan in most social settings. Hell, with his parents, it was expected. Contrary to what Laurel believed, Mac didn't have to borrow a tux for the auction because he already owned one. It was hanging in his closet along with all his other expensive suits.

Laurel made the introductions and Dylan Malone took Mac's hand in a strong handshake. Dylan narrowed his eyes. "Have we met somewhere?"

Damn. It was possible that Dylan might have seen him at Malone Financial Services. He wasn't sure if her brother had been there since Mac had been hired.

"I don't think so," Mac said convincingly enough, starting to sweat.

He scanned the club looking for potential threats. He often frequented this chi-chi West Chelsea hotspot, but thankfully no one inside looked vaguely familiar. It was also dim enough in here that it was a bit hard to fully make out features unless you were very close.

The classy space, designed by big-name architectural firm Jason Spangler was impressive. A glass-bead chandelier lit up the dramatic main room, accented by dark, polished wood on all sides and sprawling banquette seating. At the back, a pyramid-like staircase led to a soundproof, glassed-in, second-floor lounge overlooking the vaulted main room.

Laurel took his hand and they pressed through the crowd to the bar. Champagne was free-flowing and many people were drinking the bubbly stuff, but Mac needed something stronger.

"I'll have tequila, straight," he told the bartender.

Laurel said, "A French seventy-five."

She'd gone with a blend of gin, lemon juice and sugar topped off with champagne, so she wasn't feeling as much stress as Mac was, that was for sure.

Laurel turned to talk to someone and Mac heard Sherry's voice over the din of the crowd. He moved sideways by increments, getting lost amid the partygoers. He found a dim and secluded place where he could watch Laurel and Sherry from a safe distance.

Laurel looked around for him, but shrugged and struck up a conversation with her friend. Mac's palms were moist. He shrugged out of his leather jacket and slung it on the closest banquette.

As soon as Sherry and her boyfriend moved away to the dance floor, Mac returned to Laurel.

"Mac, there you are. You just missed meeting Sherry."

"I'm sure I'll have that pleasure before the night is out," Mac said, surreptitiously keeping an eye on his assistant. When Sherry turned his way, he very effectively turned his shoulder to hide his face.

The music was beating a heavy rhythm and Mac leaned down. "Do you want to dance?"

Laurel nodded and they moved to the dance floor. It was so crowded that Mac had to move against Laurel, but he didn't mind that one bit. She was dressed in a tight black lace dress with a low-cut back and a plunging neckline. A simple black ribbon encircled her throat and diamond earrings dripped from her ears.

As the music continued, he found his eyes wandering to the sway of her tight, sexy body. He reached out and slid his hand around the slender expanse of her waist, moving his lower body closer, forcing her legs apart so that she danced her groin against his thigh. She smoothly matched her movements to his and held his gaze, hers full of excitement and pleasure.

When that number ended, a slow, sultry Latin tune played over the speakers. He gathered her against him as she rested her head against his chest.

He moved closer to her, trailed his lips down her neck as she twined her arms around his and continued to move intimately against him.

Sliding her hands to his waist then to his lower back, she splayed her palms against the muscled slope of his spine, the heat of her touch seeping through his shirt.

God, she was so damned sexy, she made his insides clench and his palms itch to touch her everywhere.

But he had to remember that they were in a public place. The music ended on a slow, provocative note. Mac saw that Sherry and Michael were moving toward Laurel. He asked, "Would you like another drink?"

Without waiting for an answer, Mac moved away toward the bar and his hiding spot.

The night progressed with Mac disappearing each time he saw Sherry coming toward Laurel. Finally, the tension was too much for him, and as Sherry and Michael went up to the soundproof room on the second-floor, Mac went outside and had the valet get his car. Back inside he looked for Laurel who was talking to her sister-in-law.

"Laurel, didn't you want to get an early start tomorrow?" Mac said when he came abreast of her.

"I did. We'd better get going." She turned to Haley. "Looks like your party was a great success."

"Thanks for coming. It was nice to see you again, Mac."

Mac nodded and steered Laurel for the door. From behind him, he heard Sherry's voice calling Laurel's name and she was getting way too close. He moved Laurel through the crowd at a quicker pace, his heart pounding.

They broke out into the street at a fast walk, Laurel rushing, but Mac didn't slow.

The valet waited beside the car and Mac opened the passenger side door, and practically shoved Laurel into the seat.

He slammed the car door and jumped into the driver's seat after giving the valet a tip.

"Geez Mac, why the hurry? That was Sherry," Laurel protested.

He roared away from the curb just as Sherry reached it and he felt a shock go through his system as Sherry met his eyes for a brief second. He replied, "I saw someone I didn't want to talk to."

Had it been enough time for her to recognize him? He sure as hell hoped not.

11

What kind of underwear would your hottie wear?

a. boxers
b. boxer briefs
c. briefs
d. nothing.

> *—Excerpt from* Who's Your Hottie? *quiz,*
> SPICE *magazine*

LAUREL PLACED HER bag behind the driver's seat of her SUV. Mac did the same.

He still hadn't asked where they were going and she didn't feel the need to elaborate.

"It's an hour away."

He turned amused eyes toward her. "I'm intrigued."

She didn't feel the need to talk mostly because her anxiety level was rising the closer they got to Cranberry. How did she talk about something so dear to her heart? How did she verbalize that she felt so connected to Mac that he was the only person in her life she trusted with this secret.

When they reached the outskirts of the little town, Laurel said, "We're almost there. I should warn you that this place is very small and quaint."

"Oh yeah?"

"I love it there. I have to make one stop before we get to where we're going."

"Okay."

"It's the lumber yard."

Mac turned to her with a stunned look on his face. "Why the lumber yard?"

"I told my neighbor I'd do some work for him in exchange for a lasagna dinner and I called him when you were in the shower to let him know I was bringing a guest. Mr. Hayes said that was great and I could invite anyone I wanted."

"I get a free dinner, too? Sweet."

She smiled at him. "The more the merrier, I say. Do you know anything about carpentry work?"

"What are we talking about?"

"Stairs."

"You know how to build stairs?"

"Yes, I do." They pulled up to the lumber yard and Laurel felt that old familiar excitement just being this close to wood. "Let's go."

She made her way through the store, picking up the items she would need. Most of the equipment she had back at her workshop.

She got to the lumber area and flagged down a clerk.

"Hi, there, Miss Malone," he said with a smile. "Back for more wood. What are you building this time?"

"I'm building outdoor stairs with seven steps, so I'll need seven finished hardwood treads and three nine-foot boards. I'll need quality grade wood and banisters. Here are all the measurements for everything. Thanks."

She paid for the wood and she could feel Mac's eyes on her.

After making her purchases, she told the guy she would pull her car around.

Mac fell into step beside her. "I'm impressed as hell. I had no idea that you knew anything about carpentry."

"Why? Because I'm a girl?"

"Uh, women can do anything, including carpentry. It's just that...it's like picking up a shiny object in the sand and discovering it's a diamond. I really like discovering things about you, Laurel."

With wry amusement still pulling at her mouth, Laurel tipped her head. "That's got to be the nicest thing anyone has ever said to me. Let's go get the wood. I'll need to get started on those stairs if I'm going to get them finished."

"Laurel, what a pleasant surprise."

"Wanda, it's nice to see you. How's the diner?"

"Busy every day. I can't cook or bake enough to keep these people happy."

Laurel turned to Mac. "Mac Hayes, meet Wanda Sanders, she owns and runs the local diner."

They exchanged pleasantries and then Laurel said, "You know, Mr. Hayes has invited us for lasagna after I fix his stairs. He said I could invite anyone I want. How about you?"

"Oh, I don't know." Wanda blushed. "I don't want to intrude."

"It won't be an intrusion. I'd love to have a chance to catch up with you."

"Maybe I will."

"What was that all about?" Mac asked as Wanda walked away.

"Mr. Hayes is sweet on her. I'm just giving them a

nudge. They've been dancing around each other for months."

"Matchmaking can be dangerous."

"Ever since I met you, I like living on the edge."

WHEN SHE PULLED into the driveway next to a little clapboard house, Mac's patience ran out. "Okay, I've waited as long as I can. Where are we?"

"This is my home away from home. See that white house. I own it."

"Your escape from the city?"

"Sort of. It's a little more than that."

Before Mac could ask her, he saw an older man cross the yard from the house next door. For a moment, the man seemed oddly familiar as if he'd seen him somewhere before.

Laurel got out of her SUV and greeted her neighbor. "Mr. Hayes. Let me introduce you to Mac Hayes. He's going to help me with your stairs."

"Glad to have you, son." The man reached out and clasped Mac's hand. He gave Mac a quizzical look. "Funny we have the same name."

Mac nodded.

They got right to unloading the lumber and brought it to the back of the house.

Laurel was not only beautiful to watch, but he found himself even in more awe of her as she began to assemble wood, frame out the stairs, and cut the stringers that would hold the treads and the risers. She worked fast and effortlessly, measuring and hammering and giving him orders he followed without comment.

It was a hot day and Mr. Hayes brought them beer and regaled them with jokes that kept them in stitches. When the stairs were done and the tools replaced, Laurel went over to the hose and cleaned herself off.

She looked at Mac with merriment in her eyes and before he could duck, she'd gotten him with a squirt of the hose right in the face. He chased her and they fought over it. That was about the time the first person arrived. Then a young girl with a pretty pink dress came by, then more—old folks and families with children in tow. All of them were carrying dishes of food. Before Mac realized what was happening, there was a yard full of people.

Mr. Hayes had started the barbecue and when Mac and Laurel approached him, he turned to them and said, "Sorry, no lasagna, Laurel, but when I let slip that you were fixing my stairs, I got all these offers from people to come over. Before I knew it, it was a potluck barbecue. I hope you don't mind."

"We don't mind, Mr. Hayes, although I will miss having your lasagna. It's delicious."

"Don't you worry about that. I made you one and put it in the refrigerator."

Shortly after that, Wanda arrived and she never left Mr. Hayes's side.

It'd been a long time since Mac had attended a barbecue and he enjoyed chatting with Laurel's neighbors and watching Laurel herself move around as if she was a hostess at a party. Always talking and laughing, full of energy and life.

When he spied her walking toward her SUV, he excused himself from the conversation about the planning for the town's Fourth of July celebration and followed her.

She was pulling a sweatshirt out of her bag when he came up behind her. "Cold?" he asked. "All you had to do was tell me. I know a few ways to warm you up."

"And all of them are illegal in public," she said, pulling the sweatshirt over her head. "Having a good time?"

"The best."

"I know it's not exactly your scene, but they're nice people."

"They are."

Someone turned on a radio and soft music filled the night. Mac looked up. "Damn those stars are beautiful. You don't get this kind of view in the city."

"That's why I like coming out here. It gives me a fresh perspective on everything. It's so simple here, no hustle and bustle, just a measured pace of life."

He carefully tucked some hair behind her ear, the feel of her oddly comforting.

He stroked her cheek with his thumb, then slid his fingers into her hair. "Everyone needs a place to go where they can rejuvenate." For him it was the Hamptons and the beautiful beach outside his parents' home. He felt completely frustrated that he couldn't tell her about them or the house he loved so much. What would a bad-boy biker know about the Hamptons or the beach? This whole disguise was beginning to chafe. He so wanted to tell her who he was and drop this whole thing, but this place of solitude and respite didn't seem like a good place. He didn't want to ruin her sense of home she had when she visited here.

"Will you look at that," Laurel said with a whisper.

Mac turned his head and felt a kick to his heart when he saw Mr. Hayes and Wanda sitting on the porch swing, talking and holding hands.

"Told you," she said smugly.

Mac couldn't resist that sassy little mouth. He leaned down and captured her lips.

After that, things broke up and Laurel and Mac headed to her small house.

Once inside, she directed him upstairs to the closest bedroom where he dropped the bags. As he was leaving the room he happened to glance into the half-open closet. On the top shelf were a number of board games. He recognized Life and Trivial Pursuit, but it was Monopoly that caught his eye.

He reached up and pulled the box down. In a few minutes he stepped into the living room where Laurel was lighting a fire to chase away the late spring chill in the air.

She looked up when he came in the room and smiled when she saw the game in his hands.

"If you're thinking of challenging me to a game of Monopoly, I have to warn you that I play to win."

"Cutthroat, huh?"

"Downright bloodthirsty."

"I wouldn't have it any other way."

"Let me make us some hot chocolate. I'll be right back."

Mac settled down in front of the fire and pulled the cover off the game. Memories of the times he'd beat the pants off Tyler made him smile. He picked up the top-hat token and set it on Go. "What token do you want?" he called to her.

"I'll take the iron."

He selected the iron and placed that too on Go.

Laurel walked into the room with two mugs emitting curls of steam. She set them on the lip of the fieldstone fireplace and sat cross-legged on the floor in front of the board. "Who's going to be the banker?"

"We'll roll for it."

He picked up the dice and threw them. One die landed on five and the other on six.

"Not bad," Laurel said, picking up the dice and throwing them, scoring two sixes.

"Something tells me I'm about to be humbled."

They played fast and furious for one and a half hours. Laurel was good. She bought Park Place and Boardwalk. She owned the utility companies and two out of the four railroads along with North Carolina Ave., Pennsylvania Ave., and Pacific Ave., the next highest rent rich properties. She'd also bought St. Charles Place, Virginia Place and States Ave., leaving him with the rest of the properties. He'd parlayed his one thousand dollar stake into three thousand, but Laurel looked like she'd doubled that.

Before her turn was over, she bought a hotel for Boardwalk and set it down with a sassy smile.

Mac rolled and moved from Ventnor Ave. to Community Chest. He picked up his card and laughed. "I collect ten bucks for second prize in a beauty contest."

Laurel reached into the money bin and pulled out ten dollars. "Maybe if you shared your Community Chest more, you'd have gotten first prize."

"I'm not that kind of guy." He took the money and added it to his stash.

Laurel rolled and landed on Chance, she picked up the Go Directly to Jail card without collecting two hundred dollars. She scowled and advanced her token to the jail.

"Hmm. Can a banker be a jailbird?"

"Sure. I can conduct my affairs from jail, just like all the other jailbirds."

Mac picked up the dice and rolled a three to land on Chance. When he picked up his card, he found a Get Out of Jail Free card.

He showed it to Laurel. "Look at this. What would you do to get out of jail free?"

"Plenty buddy, but I think I'll try my hand at rolling doubles, since all of the things I'd do are rated X."

"I'm not complaining."

"You wouldn't." She picked up the dice and rolled, ending up with a three and a one.

"Tough luck," Mac said, holding up the card. "What will you give me for it?"

"I'll do something to heat you up."

"Deal," he said. He handed over the card and Laurel moved her token out of jail.

Laurel leaned across the board and then snatched up his cup, giggling. "Okay, hot chocolate it is."

"Cheater," he called after her.

Laurel was having the time of her life as she put the kettle on to boil. Mac came up behind her, his hands stealing around her waist. His mouth dipped to the soft skin of her neck and she sighed and leaned into the kiss.

"Having fun."

"Yes, you are a tough player." She was having way too much fun with this surprisingly versatile bad boy.

One who knew how to wield a hammer, do math like he'd majored in it in college, and play Monopoly like a real estate tycoon. She was having a hard time not falling for him.

"I thought I was good. I always kicked Tyler's butt, but you, lady, are the premier Monopoly player. I offer you my crown."

"And a nice crown it is, but I haven't won yet. So don't be too quick in conceding your defeat."

The kettle whistled, and she grabbed the black handle, pouring a stream of hot water into his mug. She scooped out two heaping spoonfuls of chocolate and stirred, finally adding a handful of mini-marshmallows from an open bag on the counter.

He picked up the mug and went back to the living room to resume their play.

It was Mac's turn and he rolled a three to land on Boardwalk, netting Laurel a two thousand dollar payoff.

After several turns Laurel landed on the Income Tax square. In her haughtiest voice she said, "No taxes for us. Leave the taxes to the little people."

"Very funny. Do you want to go back to jail?"

She laughed as she paid her fair share. Finally Mac rolled and ended up on Park Place, costing him fifteen hundred dollars of which he only had twelve hundred. "I could mortgage my property."

"Or you could give me the shirt off your back and I'll call it even?"

He grinned as he popped the buttons and pulled off the shirt. The temperature seemed to go up twenty degrees.

His chest was well-defined, the firelight playing off his hard muscles.

"Laurel, it's your turn."

"Right." She picked up the dice and rolled. The next time that Mac landed on one of her properties, he was still short of cash. "I'll take the pants".

He stood up and unzipped and unsnapped his jeans. He slid the denim down, *accidentally* snagging the waistband of his underwear, revealing the tip of his hard, fully aroused cock. He inclined his head imprudently, and said, "Oops. I almost overpaid."

She could see the restrained arousal blazing in his bright blue eyes. Laurel squirmed when he slowly reached down and snagged the waistband of his briefs and pulled them back up.

"Lose the briefs."

"It's not my turn."

"No, it's mine and I say the game's over and I win. Now, didn't you say something about giving me your crown?"

His smile was full of sinful intent. "I did. What did you go to jail for, indecent proposal?"

"That's right. Why don't you come over here and make something out of it?"

"I will, but not because you want me to."

"Why then?"

"I'm a sucker for a jailbird."

He skinned the red cotton down his legs and kicked it away, then straightened, giving her the full-frontal view of him.

Completely and unabashedly nude and aroused for her, he stole her breath away.

She took in the light dusting of hair on his chest, followed the narrowing path down to his rippled belly, and lower to the most prominent, impressive part of him. She swallowed hard. His thoroughly erect cock was parallel to his stomach, pointing straight up to his navel, impossibly hard and thick.

"I'd have given you first place in that beauty contest and the grand prize," she said.

Taking a minute to arrange large pillows around the fireplace, she reached across the board and grabbed his hand, pulling him down to the floor. Without another word, she pushed him onto his stomach.

"I had plans for you tonight. Hold on just a sec."

She ran upstairs to her bag to get the edible ambrosia massage oil and quickly dressed in the red open cup bra, garter belt and stockings. The only makeup she put on was a deep red, moist lipstick. When she got back downstairs, Mac had turned to his side and propped his cheek in his hand. His slumberous eyes watched every move she made as she descended the stairs.

"Damn."

When she reached him she knelt down. "Roll back."

"I want to look at you some more," Mac said, resisting her push against his shoulder.

Laurel smiled softly. "Don't worry. You can look your fill when I let you turn around. I'm not taking this off."

"It's open in all the right places," he breathed, running his fingertip along the edge of her bra strap. "I want your silky legs wrapped around my hips as I drive into you."

"I love that."

"What?"

"Telling me what you'd like to do to me."

"Talking dirty."

"Yes."

"Like I want to put my lips on your nipples and bring you to orgasm with my mouth."

"Oh, Mac," she gasped, closing her eyes as a rush of heat scorched every nerve ending.

He sat up abruptly, grabbed her upper arms and dragged her against him, which thrust her hot, hard nipples up and close to his waiting mouth. For a moment he looked deep into her eyes, the way he drew out the anticipation made her frantic for the feel of his hot, wet mouth. His lips covered one nipple and Laurel thought she would catapult right out of her skin. His tongue lapped and swirled until he finally drew the nipple into his mouth and suckled her.

Laurel moaned, giving herself over to the delightful feel of Mac's scalding mouth on her turgid nipple, arousing her to the point of dizzying torment. Her other nipple tingled and ached, throbbing for his mouth.

Her sex felt swollen, slick with her own desire, and his illicit caress was driving her mad. She rolled her head, willing to beg for what she yearned for. "Mac, please."

With a growl he took the other nipple and Laurel cried out at the exquisite sensation tugging at her sex.

"I've never seen anything so sexy, so mouthwateringly tempting as the sight of your tits thrusting out of this bit of lace."

Laurel let him ruthlessly increase the arch of her back and she sobbed out his name.

"Stay like that, just like that," he said as he cupped both her breasts in his big hands and squeezed them together his mouth biting and sucking until she thought she'd go mad.

She came with a white-hot burst of passion that made her cry out as her hips bucked helplessly caught in a maelstrom of intense pleasure.

She fell against him weak and wrung out, shivering through the aftershocks.

When she was able to take in enough air to speak, she looked up at him. "I didn't plan that part. You always turn the tables on me."

"The unexpected really does take you places."

"I'd be more than happy to go to that place again, but now I have plans for you."

"You won't hear me argue with the Queen of Monopoly."

"Lie down face-first." He did as he was told and Laurel opened the oil and dropped a few drops into her hand. She rubbed the oil between her palms to warm it and then started on his foot, massaging the oil in until his skin was slick. The light silky oil had a sweet, delicate scent that teased her senses.

Then she climbed onto him and lowered her clit until it touched his skin. He made a hot, muffled noise as she rubbed herself against him, thrusting her swollen clit against his heel and along her lips. Taking more oil, she slathered it along his leg and moved up gliding her sex along the hard contours of his calf.

He shifted as if he wanted to turn, but she put her hands on the small of his back to keep him in place. She moved up over his buttocks riding him in an uncontrollable sexy dance. The oil made her clit tingle, the friction of his skin and the slickness of the oil a sensual torture.

Sensations as exquisite as they were intense rippled through her in undulating waves of passion, beckoning her to let go. Curling her fingers into tight fists at her sides, she continued to move sinuously on his muscular thigh until her entire body began to shake. Biting her lip, she finally took her pleasure with a soft, keening cry of release. Moving over his thigh, her silk-clad legs hugging and squeezing, she moved down his body until she reached his other heel.

As soon as she was off him, he flipped over and said hoarsely, "Ride me, Laurel. Now."

She didn't need any more coaxing as she grabbed a condom, sheathed him, and impaled herself onto his hard, pulsating cock.

His eyes flared wide in response, giving her a brief glimpse of passion, heat and something else warring in their hot blue depths. Before she could analyze that last emotion, she was moving on him, her body undulating and grinding against his as she increased her rhythmic pace.

A low throaty, on-the-edge moan escaped him, and he reared up and grabbed the back of her head crushing her mouth to his, kissing her with a desperate, fierce passion that caught her off guard. His tongue swept into her mouth, matching the rapid, pistoning stroke of her hips and the slick, penetrating slide of his flesh in hers.

Tremors radiated through her from the sensitive spot where they were joined so intimately. She felt thoroughly possessed by him, body and soul, in a way that defied their impersonal bargain and the simplicity of an affair. In a way that aroused feelings that had no business being a part of this temporary relationship.

Pushing those thoughts aside, she concentrated on the pleasure he gave her, and how alive he made her body feel. Running her hands down the slope of his spine, she grasped his waist and held on. Her orgasm broke over her like a gigantic tidal wave rushing with a power as awesome as the earth.

This time he was right there with her when she reached the peak of her climax. Groaning, he broke their kiss and tossed his head back, his hips driving hard, his body tightening, straining against hers.

And he let go.

12

What kind of light would you like to make love by?

a. chandelier
b. flashing lights
c. neon light
d. moonlight
　　　　　—Excerpt from Who's Your Hottie? *quiz,*
　　　　　　　　　　　　SPICE *magazine*

MAC WOKE TO THE dusky light of dawn, the pillows beneath him a soft bed. They hadn't even made it upstairs the night before. The Monopoly game was strewn across the living room and the fire was nothing but embers.

He closed his eyes expecting to hear morning noise in the kitchen, but it was silent. The house was silent. Where was Laurel?

He could no longer deny the feelings that he had for her. Although she thought of him as a temporary lover, he wanted her in his life. Permanently.

He was in love with her.

His heart pounded hard and fast, an adrenaline rush that swept through him as he finally put words to the emotions tumbling around in his chest. He didn't fight the sentiment, didn't deny its existence. Instead, he allowed it to flow through him and let himself get used to the feeling of knowing that this one special woman complemented him so perfectly, in ways that made him feel whole and complete, physically and emotionally.

He realized that it was now coming down to days as to when he would tell her who he was and how he came to be involved with her. From the beginning he'd wanted to be honest with her. But how would she take it? How would she react to the fact that he was exactly the type of man she couldn't see herself with? He knew why.

Her role model had been her father and she measured everyone up to him. To her all stockbrokers were cut from the same cloth. He'd have to show her that her generalizations were wrong in his case. He'd learned a little about himself in the last couple of weeks. He was a bit of a rebel inside and he could embrace that.

Mac pushed back the blanket Laurel must have gotten for them last night and dressed. He looked around the house but couldn't find her anywhere.

Pulling on a sweatshirt against the early morning chill, he stepped out of the house and looked around. Laurel wasn't anywhere to be seen. Had she taken a walk? It was a glorious day.

He heard a metallic sound from the detached garage. Approaching it, he opened the side door quietly. Light from the skylights filtered inside. Laurel was at a workbench using a tool to smooth out a mitered piece of wood. Plans were tacked above her head, sketched out with dimensions and other information written in the margins.

She was dressed in a pair of jean overalls and a white

tank top made more dazzling by the sunlight. She wore
work boots on her feet and her dark hair was pulled into
a tight ponytail.

Mac stood there and watched her work as it slowly
dawned on him. This was her secret. She was the craftsperson behind the bedroom set in her room, the lip
chair, the mosaic table and the interesting art pieces on
the walls. Laurel was a skilled furniture designer and
builder.

He could see right away why she was hiding this
from her father. Her traditional father would never approve of this kind of off-beat pursuit.

But it was much more than that and Mac saw what
was at the crux of Laurel's anxiety. She was trying to
live up to her mother's expectations. This furniture was
a way for her to express not only her inner creativity,
but the gift her mother had unwittingly given her daughter. It made a lot of things clear to him, but obviously
they weren't clear to her. A thousand feelings piled up
in his chest. Guilt, uncertainty, self-doubt, fear, but
most of all love.

Feeling suddenly very shaky inside, he entered the
garage. Laurel turned at the sound. It pulled at his heart
the look of vulnerability on her face.

"This is your secret?"

She nodded and put down the tool, taking off her safety
glasses and laying them beside the tool. "No one knows."

"Why, Laurel?"

She shrugged and stepped away from him, her gaze
on the numerous finished pieces in the back of the garage. "They wouldn't understand."

"You mean your father wouldn't approve."

"God, no. He would not approve of me spending a penny on this place. He would look at my furniture and just not get it just like he didn't get my mother's collection."

He walked over to her and cupped her cheek, turning her toward him. "It's not all about your father."

"What is it about? Enlighten me."

"You're afraid to expose yourself to everyone, not just your family."

"It's just furniture."

"I think it's much more than that, Laurel. It's part of your identity. What you love to do and you don't want it scrutinized, held up to your mother's achievement and measured. That's why you acted so anxious every time someone gushed about your mother. That woman, Mrs. Foster. She said you were very like your mother."

Laurel stubbornly shook her head. "I'm protecting myself by keeping this place quiet, that's true," she said, staring up at him. "Just like I try to protect myself from getting hurt. Until I met you, that is."

He tried to smile as he stroked her cheek with his thumb. "Your little piece of heaven," he said, his voice gruff.

"But I was able to show it to you. What does that say?"

"It says that you trust me."

She stared at him for an instant longer; then she closed her eyes and came into his arms, holding on to him with desperate strength. Closing his own eyes, Mac roughly buried his face in her neck, locking his arms around her. Inhaling raggedly, he tightened his hold on her, an agony of guilt rushing through him.

"I do. I really do."

It took him a while, but he got himself under control and could finally breathe without that hard ache in his chest. Releasing a shaky sigh, he adjusted his hold on her, drawing her deeper into his embrace, his lungs constricting. The thought of her working out here all alone sobered him like little else had, and he pressed her hard against him, a dozen regrets settling deep in his heart. If only...If only...

Knowing that kind of thinking wouldn't help, he simply held her, the fullness in his chest expanding. She was so strong and so vulnerable. She felt so good and smelled so good.

Unable to control the urge, he widened his stance a little, pressing her against the hard ridge of flesh, turning his face against her neck and clenching his teeth.

She made a low desperate sound and twisted her head, her mouth suddenly hot and urgent against his. The bolt of pure, raw sensation knocked the wind right out of him. Mac shuddered, and he widened his mouth against hers, feeding on the desperation that poured back and forth between them. She made another wild sound and clutched at him, the movement welding their bodies together like two halves of a whole, and he nearly lost it right then. But the taste of her was erotic and he ground his mouth down onto hers.

Wrong. This was wrong. He was supposed to tell her who he was, not have sex with her again. But he wanted her and knew when those words crossed his lips everything would change and he couldn't seem to let go of her.

She clutched him tighter, already sensing that he

was going to pull away, as if she were trying to climb right inside him. Her arms locked around Mac, she choked out his name; then she moved against him, silently pleading with him, pleading with her body and any connection he had with reason shattered into a thousand pieces.

The feel of her heat against him was too much, and he clenched his jaw. His face contorting from the surge of desire, he caught her around the hips welding her roughly against him. He needed this—the heat of her, the weight of her. Her. He needed her.

Laurel made another low sound, then she inhaled raggedly and pulled herself up against his arousal, her voice breaking on a low sob of relief. "Mac, don't stop. Please don't stop." She moved against him again, and Mac tightened his hold even more, unable to stop as he involuntarily responded. Body to body, heat to heat, and suddenly there was no turning back.

Shifting her head, he covered her mouth in a hot, deep kiss, and she opened to him, her mouth moving against his with an urgent hunger. It was too much and not nearly enough, and Mac lifted her higher and caught her behind the knee, dragging her leg around his hip. With one twisting motion, his hard heat was flush against hers. Grasping her buttocks, he thrust against her again and again, a low groan wrenched from him as she moved with him, riding him, riding the hard thick ridge jammed against her. But that wasn't enough, either. Mac nearly went ballistic, certain he would burst if he didn't get inside her.

Making incoherent sounds against his mouth, Laurel twisted free and a violent shudder coursed through

Mac when he felt her hands fumble with the snap, then the zipper, on his pants. The instant she touched his hard throbbing flesh, he groaned out her name and let go of her, desperate to rid them both of the barrier of clothes.

Somehow he got her overalls off, and her shirt pulled over her head, but the instant he felt her hand close around him, he lost it completely. Jerking her hand away, he hauled her up against him. On the verge of release, he dragged her legs around him again, then backed her against the workbench. Wedging his arm between her and the roughened wood, he clenched his eyes shut and thrust into her, unable to hold back one second longer. The feel of her, tight and wet, closing around him drove the air right out of him, the sensation so intense he couldn't move.

Laurel locked her legs around him, her movements urging him on, and Mac crushed her against him, white-hot desire rolling over him. Angling his arm across her back, he drove into her again and again pressure building and building. A low guttural sound was torn from him, and his release came in a blinding rush that went on and on, so powerful he felt as if he were being turned inside out. He wanted to let it roll over him, to take him under, but he forced himself to keep moving in her, knowing she was on the very edge. She cried out and clutched at his back, then went rigid in his arms, and she finally convulsed around him, the gripping spasms wringing him dry.

His heart hammering, his breathing so labored he felt almost dizzy, he weakly rested his head against hers, his whole body quivering. He felt as if he had been wrenched in two.

He didn't know how long he stood there, with her trembling in his arms, not an ounce of strength left in him.

It wasn't until he shifted his hold and tucked his face against hers that he realized her cheek was wet with tears. Hauling in an unstable breath, he turned his head and kissed her on the neck, a feeling of overwhelming protectiveness rising up his chest. Yet the only person he really needed to protect her from was him.

He was acutely aware of how important this moment was in time. Laurel trusted him with a significant part of her life.

He waited a moment for the knot of emotion to ease; then he smoothed his hand up her back. "Can you hang on for a minute?" he asked thickly.

She nodded once and tightened her arms and legs around him. Mac withdrew his arms from around her back and supported her buttocks enough for her to release her hold and slide down until her feet touched the concrete.

They dressed quickly, the early morning chill cooling the sweat on their bodies.

When they were done, he pulled her toward him. Inhaling unevenly, he covered her mouth with a soft, searching kiss, trying to give her something he wasn't sure what. An apology? She'd given of herself to a man who'd been false to her. Her breath caught when he deepened the kiss with slow, lazy thoroughness. Working his mouth softly, slowly against hers, he drank from her, probing the moist recesses, savoring the taste of her.

His hand tangled into her silky hair. His chest tightening. "Laurel, I love it that you trust me, but you need to trust yourself, too. Your furniture should be part of that auction."

Laurel recoiled and said, "No!"

His hand not quite steady, he could barely hold her hand, the lump in his throat so intense it made his jaws ache. He didn't know what he would do if she walked out of his life forever, but this was too important for him to back down because she didn't want to hear what he had to say.

"Why not, Laurel. Look at this stuff." He walked over to the deep-blue sofa with the silver circles on it and ran his hand along the square back. Next, he squatted and examined the arm of a chair. "Look at this joint, it's flawless, unless you look closely it looks like one piece of endless wood."

"Mac, you're wasting your breath. I'm not good enough to enter that auction. The designers and craftsmen have been at it for years. They studied—"

"Who gives a damn, Laurel? You're fooling and cheating yourself as well as people who would admire and be proud to put a piece of your furniture in their homes. This right here is the most profound legacy to your mother." He walked up to her. "You are a living, breathing legacy."

She turned away, her face closed, a stubborn set to her jaw. "I'm not doing it. So, you can just drop it. You're wrong about it all. I don't want to take a risk because I'm afraid, pure and simple. I don't have what it takes."

There was nothing more he could say. He stayed

mute until they got outside of the garage and headed for the house.

He realized in that moment that he had to tell her. He couldn't wait. Even though he'd formed them in his head, still, the words stuck in his throat and he opted to build up to his confession. "I know how it is to love a place as much as you do."

"You do?"

"My parents have a place in the Hamptons. We spent all our summers there. I loved it. The beach, the house, the lazy family time."

"The Hamptons?"

There was a sudden wariness in her voice as if it unnerved her they were on the same social scale. Not what she wanted from her bad-boy stud.

"Yes, my parents are wealthy. My father is a real estate developer."

"That's it," she said softly. "The manners, the inborn confidence you possess. I couldn't quite put my finger on it."

"There's a reason why I seem like I'm two different guys...."

"Laurel, Mac. Come over and have some blueberry pancakes."

Laurel waved at Mr. Hayes. "Come on. Mr. Hayes makes the best blueberry pancakes in the State of New York." She walked past him, leaving him in her wake and the words he was about to utter died on his lips.

Laurel didn't notice. The emotions in her too much for her to sort through. He had to be wrong about all that he said. Her furniture wasn't good enough to be auctioned at the Met in her mother's wing of the museum.

She pushed away his argument that she was reacting to the fact that she was trying to live up to her mother's reputation. Laurel wasn't anything like her mother.

She stopped short and thought about that as the words reverberated in her head. It was true. She wasn't like her mother at all.

They made their way up the stairs into Mr. Hayes's living room and Mac followed Mr. Hayes into the kitchen, but Laurel stopped dead staring at a photograph sitting on the mantel of the fireplace.

The world seemed to move out of kilter as she stared at the photograph. She'd seen it before. The very same photograph, only larger, hung on Mac's bedroom wall. Could this be Tyler and their mother?

"Come sit in the kitchen," Mr. Hayes said close to her shoulder. "That's a picture of my ex-wife and my son. We were divorced a long time ago."

Mr. Hayes looked at the photo and traced the laughing faces of the woman and child. "We all used to live in this house. After the divorce, I took off for California to live in a commune. The house was mine. I bought out my ex-wife's share. I could never bear to sell it. Later, I lost track of them, but I retired here because it made me feel closer to them, to the happiest part of my life."

"Why did you leave?"

"My wife told me something shocking about herself and I couldn't handle it. Couldn't forgive her for lying to me."

Mr. Hayes shook his head. "It doesn't matter anymore. I'm not sure why it mattered so much then and I have deep regrets." He set the photograph onto the mantel and turned toward the kitchen. "But it was a long time ago."

Mr. Hayes paused then faced Laurel. "I have some wisdom for you. If you love that young man in the kitchen, never let him go and let him know every day how you feel."

He continued onto the kitchen, saying, "We'd better hurry before Mac eats up all the pancakes."

MAC DECIDED WHILE he was eating Mr. Hayes's pancakes, he would take another stab at telling Laurel who he was. Laurel seemed unsettled, but that was understandable after the argument they'd had over her submitting pieces to be auctioned off at her mother's memorial. Her hands trembled, when she picked up her fork, and Mac reached under the table and rubbed her thigh. Laurel jumped, but threw him a weak smile.

There was a knock at the door and Mr. Hayes went to answer it. Mac smiled when he heard Wanda's voice.

"Mac, I have to show you something."

She got up from the table and he followed her into the living room. Mr. Hayes had gone onto the front porch and had closed the door for a more private conversation.

She pointed out the photograph and Mac swallowed hard. He knew the people in it. One was his brother Tyler when he'd been a baby. The other person was his mother.

Mac and Tyler had both loved this photo of their laughing mother in a big floppy hat so much so, she'd blown it up for both of them and had it framed. One sat in his living room, in his loft. Another hung on the wall in Tyler's bedroom.

This was Tyler's father. It was almost more than Mac could take in.

"Mac, is Mr. Hayes your father?"

"Laurel, it's too complicated to go into here." He glanced toward the porch. "It's not what you think."

"Oh, I see. I can spill my guts, but when it comes to you, you don't want to talk about it."

"Laurel, that's not it."

"Sure," Laurel said coldly.

Mac bit off his next words, praying that she wouldn't say anything to Mr. Hayes, who walked back in the room with Wanda in tow. "Look who decided to join us for breakfast," he said beaming.

LAUREL INSISTED THAT they leave after breakfast. She said that she was starting to worry about all the preparations for the auction and she really needed to get home.

Mac didn't argue.

They didn't speak all the way back to Manhattan. Laurel fumed and drove as fast as she could. He realized with a sinking feeling in the pit of his stomach, she wanted to get away from him. He was sure she thought he was being distant and unapproachable. He couldn't deal with it right now anyway. He was too shell-shocked at what he had learned to respond to her. How would he tell Tyler what he'd found out? How would his brother respond? Should he keep the information to himself? After all, Tyler hadn't ever said he wanted to find his father or talk to him.

Mac had sympathy for Mr. Hayes. He'd talked openly about his ex-wife and son at breakfast. Mac didn't condone what he had done, but it sounded like he truly felt he'd made a mistake.

Mac was overwhelmed with emotion and wasn't really adept at handling any of it at this point.

He was in love with Laurel. But his brother meant a lot to him and he had to come to terms with this before he spoke to Tyler. He didn't want to bring up painful memories, but he just couldn't hold on to this information.

Mac thought about calling his mother, but discarded the idea. He didn't know how he really felt about his mother's other life. Sure he'd known about it. But it was weird to meet the man she'd been married to and find out that he wasn't as much of a villain as Tyler made him out to be.

It could have been a reaction on Tyler's part to protect himself. If his dad was such a bastard and left him, it would be easier to accept than his dad being a decent guy who couldn't handle a situation in his married life.

When Laurel drove up to Tyler's apartment, Mac felt downright irritable. He hated the information he possessed. He hated the stupid disguise he had to wear. Right now he could really use Laurel's advice. So when he said goodbye to her it came out rough.

"Look, Mac. Maybe it would be better if we cooled it for a while," Laurel said, her shoulders rigid.

"What is that supposed to mean."

"It was fun, but I need a man who can express himself, not take all I have to give and give nothing back."

"Laurel, that's not what I'm doing."

"You're not being straightforward at all. You know so much about me, but I know so little about you."

"Laurel, don't do this. Not now. I do need you."

"I'm sorry," she said, waiting for him to close the door.

He did, but came around to the driver's side and Laurel's open window. Mac couldn't let her go. "Let me call you tomorrow."

"Do you expect me to believe that? I know guy-speak when I hear it." She stared straight ahead.

"That's not fair. I've never treated you badly. Don't start a fight now."

She turned toward him. "I care about you, but you won't let me in and maybe that's some kind of bad-boy thing, but it's not for me."

"I just need a little space." The words came out of his mouth before he could stop them. He had so much on his mind that he couldn't deal with her. He was in a deep hole, one he'd dug for himself. If he told her, he would lose her, but not telling her wasn't an option, either.

He had to tell her and it had to be soon.

"Oh my God. That particular guyspeak I know."

Before Mac could say another word, she put the SUV into gear and sped off.

Mac couldn't handle seeing Tyler then, so he caught a cab home. The heaviness inside him unbearable. He climbed the stairs to his loft and walked directly to his bedroom and sat on the bed and stared at the picture atop his dresser.

His mother laughing with a cute, chubby Tyler in her arms, that big floppy hat with the flowers. She looked so happy and carefree.

He sat and looked at that picture for a long time.

LAUREL SLAMMED INTO her brownstone and chucked her luggage so hard it slid all the way to the bottom of the stairs.

"Give me my space. I'll give you some space."

Why couldn't he have been honest and just told her how he was feeling? It's exactly how she imagined her father would react—closemouthed and irritable. It still shocked her that he was from the same social strata as her father. How could she have deluded herself so badly?

Of all the nerve. He'd taken her in the sun in her workshop and, at the time, she thought they had connected deeply, but maybe it had all been one-sided. It was as if he'd touched her soul in the garage, a melding poignant interlude that she would never forget as long as she lived.

Then the silence and the moodiness. She didn't like it. She wanted a man who could communicate his feelings and thoughts and wants and needs. Mac just wasn't right for her. She should have seen that a while ago.

She bit her lip. Okay, so she was partly reacting to her anger and partly to the fact that she was frightened at the intensity of her feelings for him.

The bombshell that he was the son of a wealthy real estate developer had thrown her. It made him suitable. Her father couldn't argue with his pedigree no matter how much he didn't like the package.

The truth of the matter was that Mac thought nothing of blowing off his job, wasn't an ambitious ladder climber, and didn't give a damn what was expected of him.

Laurel had to be honest with herself. Although she wanted to dictate her own life and be her own woman, she wanted certain things and she was punctual and trustworthy and wouldn't ever think about blowing off her job. She wouldn't have it for long if she did.

But Mac worked for a tolerant brother and had the luxury of living his own kind of lifestyle. Although there were jarring idiosyncratic personality shifts, she just didn't understand. The dinner was a perfect example. He'd taken her to a ritzy restaurant and paid with a credit card. He'd taken her for a sweet, mundane bicycle ride through the park, and he'd endured Nine Inch Nails for her, snagging her difficult-to-get, expensive tickets.

He was a jumble of strange interesting characteristics that kept her guessing. Do The Unexpected seemed to be his motto. A man who kept her off-guard, a man whom she could love.

Or was it that she'd already fallen?

Hard.

Maybe, just maybe, she was reacting to that most of all.

MAC LEFT TYLER'S APARTMENT, knowing that he had to see his brother. When he got to Hayes Cycles, he made his way into the back of the shop. Tyler was directing two of his employees in the loading of the truck for the motorcycle rally tomorrow.

"Are you competing?" Mac asked when his brother spied him.

"Yes, I'm entered in a couple of races to show off the new Ducati and to advertise Hayes Cycles."

"How are you enjoying my loft?"

"The cleaning lady caught me in the shower yesterday. Saw me bare-assed naked. Screamed like a crazy woman until I told her that I was your brother. I laughed like hell when she was gone. She doesn't know I speak

Spanish and she had some interesting words to say about my dick."

"You scared the hell out of Mrs. Lopez? Geez, now I'll have to call her. She's the best cleaning lady I've ever had."

"Speaking of the best you ever had. Am I going to get my apartment back any time soon?"

"This was your idea, Ty."

"I know. What's going on with the chick?"

"*Laurel.* We had a fight. I don't know what's going to happen, but she's one of a kind and I love her."

"That's deep."

"I was just thinking that."

"Whatever happens, man. I'm here for you."

"I know that, Ty. Thanks."

Tyler nodded his head. Mac shifted and rubbed the back of his neck, tension deep in his shoulders. "There's something I need to tell you and I'm not sure how you're going to take this, but here goes. I know where your father is."

Tyler's eyes narrowed and his lips thinned, he asked, "How? Where?"

"Laurel has a country house in a little town called Cranberry. She lives next door to him. Talk about truth being stranger than fiction."

Tyler's hands were shaking as he jammed them into his pockets. "Yeah." He tried to laugh it off, but his laugh came out forced.

"How do you feel about this?" Mac asked.

"I don't feel anything."

"Come on, man. I'm your brother. You can tell me anything."

"Look, drop it. I really don't want to discuss my old man or my feelings on the matter. He left us and it's done with."

"But maybe he had his reasons, Tyler. There are always two sides to every story."

Tyler blew out a ragged breath. "Are you actually telling me that you're on his side? That's low."

"No. I'm not on his side. I'm on yours. I just don't think you should throw away an opportunity to speak with him."

"No. Now drop it. We've got motorcycles to load and trucks to pack. Are you going to help, or stand there and harp?"

"I'll help anyway I can," Mac said, hoping his brother understood that those words were an open invitation.

As Mac loaded, his thoughts drifted back to Laurel and his problem with her. After this encounter with his brother, he felt dread snake up his spine. Sometimes love wasn't enough to help someone understand what they needed to do. He would tell her and accept the consequences of his own actions.

Even if that meant losing her.

13

*If your hottie wants to bind you to make love,
what's your preference:*

a. silken scarves
b. leather cuffs
c. handcuffs
d. his hands

                        —Excerpt from Who's Your Hottie? *quiz,*
                                       SPICE *magazine*

MONDAY MORNING MAC WAS at his desk early. He'd
woken up before his alarm and was unable to go back
to sleep, so he decided to get a head start on the day.

Regardless of how they had left it on Saturday, Mac
smiled softly to himself remembering his time with
Laurel.

"Wow, you must have had quite a weekend."

Sherry stood in the doorway, her hand on her hip and
a knowing light in her eyes.

"Why do you say that?"

She raised a disdaining eyebrow. "The secret smile
you have on your face. Care to share?"

Did she know? Had she recognized him at POSH?

He wasn't going to jump to any conclusions and blow it. He'd just bluff his way through it.

He dredged up a smile. "It was a mundane weekend. Not very interesting."

"Really. I find that hard to believe," she said as she walked into his office and ran her hand along the black leather of one of his visitor's chairs.

"Are you beating around the bush, Sherry?"

"It was you. Wasn't it?"

"Where?"

"Don't play dumb. I saw you driving away from POSH with Laurel. You went after her. I have to give you points for having the balls to scam her."

"I'm not scamming her."

"No? You have an alter ego—*Mac*. Just what the hell is going on between you and Laurel?"

Even though he knew this was coming, his stomach lurched.

"It's not what you think."

"And what do I think? Enlighten me."

And so he did, filling her in on the whole story from the beginning.

"Oh, God. You may have wrecked any real chance you had with Laurel."

"Only if she finds out from another source. I have to explain it to her myself. You can't tell her."

"She's my friend," Sherry said as she turned on her heel and headed for the door.

Mac came out of his seat and grabbed her arm. "Sherry, wait. Give me a minute to explain. I have really important reasons why you shouldn't."

She looked at him, her eyes dark with skepticism. "I'm listening. What are these reasons?"

"It's going to be a shock for her to hear it. She has that big presentation and the auction tomorrow. It's important that I wait until she's more relaxed. I think the explanation should come from me."

"Those are good reasons."

"I have another one."

"Spill it."

"I love her."

For a moment Sherry stared at him, sizing him up, weighing his answer. Her eyes softened and her tight shoulders loosened. "You make it very difficult to dislike you."

"I promise I'm going to tell her on Tuesday night. How do you think she'll react?"

"She's going to freak out. You'll have to be prepared for that. She doesn't know you're a stockbroker, you work in her father's firm, and you deceived her."

Mac let out a rush of air. "I know, but I felt I wouldn't have a chance if I didn't deceive her."

"Doesn't make it right."

"No, it makes it a desperate move of a desperate man. I had to meet her."

"Laurel is one of the sweetest people I know, Mr. Tolliver. I think it'll be okay."

"My friends call me Mac."

Sherry nodded. "You might not have gone about it the right way, but your heart was in the right place."

"I know I messed up, but I have to be the one to fix it. I'm asking you to please hold off. That's all."

"You really love her?" Sherry asked, the resolve in her voice weakening.

"Yes. I really do."

Sherry was silent a moment. "You've always treated me fairly and I think you're a good person. So, good luck, Mac. I hope it works out for you, but if it doesn't, I'll be there for her." The phone rang and Sherry left his office to pick it up.

Mac spied Mr. Malone heading down the hall toward Mac's office. He braced himself to meet the stern man that was Laurel's father.

"Ted," Mr. Malone said, nodding his head in acknowledgement.

"Mr. Malone. What can I do for you?"

"I got a call from Kevin Coyle. He'd like us to meet with him at ten thirty today. Any problem with that?"

"No, sir." He breathed a sigh of relief, thankful that Laurel had her meeting tomorrow morning. There was no chance they would cross paths.

"Good."

"Ms. Black," he said as he passed Sherry.

After Mr. Malone left, Mac went to the window and looked out at the New York City skyline. He bet Laurel *would* freak out. She might be a mild-mannered woman, but she had a temper when pushed. He'd say he was going to push her. He couldn't blame her if she did go up one side and down the other. He had lied to her and damn it, but he just couldn't seem to feel as sorry about it as he should.

Mostly because he had discovered an adventurous streak inside him that had been dormant. He loved riding motorcycles and mixing it up in bed. He'd had an incredible time with her, found the woman of his dreams, wanted to spend the rest of his life with her. It scared him that he might lose it all, panic washed through him, making his pulse run thick and heavy.

His thoughts went back to the way they had made love in the garage. The minute he had touched her, it had been like quicksand—once he was in, there was no damned way he could get out. But what made his gut clench even more was knowing that she could believe it was nothing more than part of the fling with her bad boy. But it wasn't. It had been more than that. One hell of a lot more.

She had held nothing back, and what she had given him had been real—her passion, her need. She had been with him every step of the way; there was no doubt in his mind about that. If she chose to walk away and he lost her, the memory of what they had shared would haunt him for a long time to come. He didn't know if it was guilt or regret, but his throat closed up every time that image took shape in his mind, and the hollow feeling in his chest spread a little more.

He wished he could talk to her today, but he had to wait until tomorrow. It was going to be a long forty-eight hours before he finally gave her his confession.

He could only hope that she could forgive him.

LAUREL HAD NEVER FELT so alone and miserable in her entire life, even while being surrounded with colleagues and clients at Waterford Scott. She'd kept her mind and hands busy all day yesterday in an attempt to work off the restless, anxious, edgy feeling that had settled within her since she'd driven away from Mac on Saturday morning.

But Monday morning hadn't dawned any brighter and she sat at her desk and brooded. She took a sip of the coffee she'd picked up downstairs and almost spilled it down the front of her blouse when the sudden ringing of the phone jarred her hand.

"Yes," Laurel said to Kelly, her assistant.

"Susan Hamilton is on the line for you."

"Put her through," Laurel instructed.

As soon as the line clicked, Laurel said, "Hello Susan, what can I do for you?"

"I'm sorry to give you such short notice, but Kevin and I have to go out of town this afternoon for an emergency meeting in London and I'm afraid we'll need you to pitch your presentation to us as soon as you can get here. Will that be a problem?"

"No. I'm fully prepared."

"Thank you. We don't want to postpone the meeting since we need an accounting firm, and we're just not sure when we'll be back from London."

"I'll see you soon."

She gathered up the papers and hastily set them in her briefcase. It took her moments to get down to the lobby of the building. Just at that moment, Mr. Scott was walking through the revolving doors and Laurel hesitated, but couldn't give up this opportunity to talk with him.

"Mr. Scott, could I speak with you."

"Yes, Laurel."

"Mr. Herman told me that you overruled his decision to promote Mark Dalton."

He frowned and nodded.

"He said that you insisted that I be promoted instead. Could you tell me why?"

He cleared his throat and looked away.

"I don't have nearly as much experience as Mark or a proven track record."

"Laurel, this is best handled in my office. Not in the lobby."

"I don't have time. I have that presentation at Coyle and Hamilton."

He sighed. "I guess you're not aware that I went to school with your father."

"My father?" Then it dawned on her. "You promoted me because my father asked you to?"

"Yes."

"I've got to go," she said abruptly. She couldn't afford to let this throw her. She had to get herself under control.

She didn't give Mr. Scott a chance to say anything else because the shock of hearing that her father had meddled in her work life was inconceivable to her. Sure, he was adamant about giving her advice, but as far as she knew, he'd never actually done anything like this.

She hailed a cab and took the time to compose herself. She would talk to him about this and express her outrage to him once she'd calmed down.

Laurel closed her eyes. Yes, that's what her mother had done. Waited until all the ugly emotions had passed then she would calmly and rationally lay out her concerns and arguments.

At the reception desk for Coyle and Hamilton, she was greeted warmly by Susan Hamilton, who ushered her to the plush conference room and Laurel gave herself over to the presentation completely.

She presented her unitedthinking concept effectively

showcasing what Waterford Scott could do for Coyle and Hamilton. At the end of the presentation, Susan smiled and rose.

"Laurel, it's our pleasure to award Waterford Scott our business."

Kevin Coyle stood and shook Laurel's hand. "Welcome aboard. I've got a meeting I have to run to, but thanks again for coming on such short notice."

Laurel waited for the sense of satisfaction and triumph to overwhelm her, but although she was happy, nothing could compare to how she felt after she'd finished a piece of her furniture and this feeling was mediocre to that.

As the attendees began to file out of the conference room, Laurel realized that what she was doing with her life wasn't as important or rewarding as working with her hands. It didn't come close to the sheer, almost spiritual feeling of creating.

In that instant, Laurel wanted that storefront on 27th Street, she wanted to fill those windows with her creations. Her mother had wanted her to be fulfilled. That's why she left her so much money to do with as she wished. This was her opportunity to honor that wish.

She wasn't her mother. That was true. She had to stop trying to be like her and be herself. Her mother wouldn't have carried on a relationship with a tough, sensitive bad boy. But Mac suited her; she was going to go to him and tell him that she loved him.

Saying the words to herself seemed to break down the wall she'd built up against it. Now she knew the reason she'd picked a fight with Mac. He was getting too close and she had been running scared.

She loved Mac Hayes and she was going to tell him so.

She realized that it was her own life and that she should direct it as she saw fit. She intended to do just that.

With those liberating thoughts, she picked up her briefcase and stepped into the hall. She spied her father talking to Kevin Coyle and a man who had an achingly familiar build. Silently she appreciated his lean, rock-solid body and the confident way he held himself. The dark blue jacket accentuated his broad shoulders. He was impeccably groomed, but there was a rugged edge to him, as familiar as her own face.

Drawn down the hall, she walked closer to the charismatic man. Suddenly her breathing deepened, her body responded with warmth and a sizzle that played along her nerve endings like fire. She swallowed to wet her dry throat.

Sexual chemistry.

Hot temptation.

It was inside her, making her insides feel on fire, increasing her steps.

Her father saw her and beckoned her over. But she would have come anyway. She had to see that man's face, knowing instinctively that he would have a sensuous mouth, his eyes would be heartbreaking, eyes that could reach out and touch her soul.

But she couldn't see any of his face since he was turned away from her, conversing with Kevin.

She reached them, willing the man to turn toward her. Her father took her arm in a gentlemanly fashion and clapped a hand to the man's expensively-clad shoulder.

"Laurel, meet Ted Tolliver, newly hired from a rival firm."

The introduction was lost on her as he shifted to meet her. Her breath caught in her throat and she dropped her briefcase. It snapped open and her papers, cell phone and pens scattered across the carpet.

"Laurel," Mac said.

Her Mac. Her motorcycle-riding, tattoo-wearing, leather-clad biker. At first, she was so disoriented she couldn't say a word. Then her father's words sank in. "...newly hired." Oh God, he was one of her father's employees.

She dropped to the rug and frantically shoveled her items back into her briefcase.

Mac bent down to help her, but Laurel slapped his hands away.

"Laurel, I can explain," he said, agony in his eyes.

She rose. Softly, she addressed her father, "It's bad enough you have to mess around in my professional life, but now you're missing around in my love life. Dad, how could you?"

"Laurel? What's the matter?" her father asked.

But she was already backing up, looking from her father to the man she'd bared her soul to, a man from the enemy's camp. It was clear. He had joined forces with her father. If she wouldn't kowtow to him by dating an upstanding guy in his office, her father would invent a man to pretend to be wild and sweet and oh-so-desirable. All those idiosyncratic characteristics fell into place like intricately cut pieces of a puzzle. The manners, the confidence, the concert tickets, everything had been staged.

"I cannot believe this. You're in this together."

"What..." her father started to say, but he was drowned out by Mac.

"Laurel...please let me explain."

"Let you explain? I don't have to let you do anything. That's what I've learned from you."

She turned on her heel and walked quickly down the hallway. Tears burned at the back of her throat. Don't let him see you cry, she told herself sternly even as the tears welled in her eyes, blurring the gold metal of the elevator doors.

She didn't know how she got down to the lobby, but the cab at the door already had passengers, with more lined up waiting. She turned away and headed down the street.

He caught up to her as she passed an alley. He grabbed her around the waist and manhandled her into a small alcove, giving them privacy.

"Laurel, let me explain."

"Go ahead and explain, Mac or should I call you Ted. What a fool I am," she said her voice filled with an edge she'd never heard before.

"It was the only way I could meet you."

"I never thought my father would ever stoop this low, but you were the perfect bait and so good at your deception. Both of you think you can manhandle me, but you can't."

"What are you talking about?"

"Don't act dumb with me. He put you up to this and you know it. *I know it.*"

"That's not true, Laurel."

"You expect me to believe a word that comes out of your mouth. You lying bastard."

"I did not plan this with your father. It has to do with that stupid test you took."

"What test?"

"That Hottie quiz. You dropped it."

"You'll stoop to amazing levels, Mac."

"No. That's not it. I saw you at the office and Sherry said you wouldn't give me the time of day. I would have done anything to meet you. When you came into Hayes Cycles with Sherry, Tyler let you believe I was what I looked to be. I went along with it. You wouldn't even look at me in the office, but at the dealership you couldn't take your eyes off me. I know it was stupid, letting you believe that I'm someone I'm not, but I had to meet you."

"I think you cooked up this scheme with my father using that test and now that it's backfired, you've come up with a nice little story. That's really awful." She swallowed hard feeling raw and provoked.

"No, Laurel. I love you. As each moment passed, I fell harder. I found it more difficult to tell you. I should have. I know. Please forgive me."

"And I love Mac Hayes, but I don't know who you are. I can't believe a word you say. You're a fake and you tricked me."

"It might have started out that way, but I found out things about myself and discovered an adventurous soul. It was me in Central Park, in bed, in that damn garage in Cranberry."

"Don't try to play on my sympathies. How can I ever forgive you for deceiving me?"

Everything changed about him. His eyes hardened, his mouth toughened, and that edge she'd seen in the hallway got dangerous. "Do you even know what you want, Laurel?" He flattened his hands on either side of her head, leaning in so close she could see the heat in his eyes—and his frustration as if he couldn't understand her reaction and was hurt that she doubted him. "Do you want a tough, doesn't-care-about-your-feelings man? I can give you that."

His hips pinned her to the wall, and she couldn't help the heated gasp that escaped her lips.

She grabbed him and kissed his mouth, her lips relentless, set to devastate. This dark seduction was even more exciting then anything he'd done to her. He moaned into her mouth.

She broke the kiss. "I know exactly what I want, but you're not that man. You never were. My parents have always tried to control me and I've let them. But no more. It was all a scheme to bring me to heel. Well, I won't. It's ironic, but you taught me to stand up for myself and take a risk."

"Laurel, please," he pleaded.

Tears threatened, but with sheer willpower, she pushed them away, her heart breaking. She couldn't love a man who betrayed her, yet she loved him so much it hurt.

Laurel pushed at his chest and stepped away from him. "Thanks for the education."

It was only after she'd gotten far enough away and was sure he hadn't followed her that she let the tears flow.

14

How would you spend quality time with your hottie?

a. watching videos curled up on the couch
b. make love all night long
c. a rousing boxing match
d. an upscale dance club
> —*Excerpt from* Who's Your Hottie? *quiz,*
> SPICE *magazine*

AFTER LEAVING MAC and gaining some composure, Laurel went back to work. She stopped briefly in her office, sat at her computer and typed, her vision often blurred by tears. Printing out the letter, she headed straight for Mr. Scott's suite.

Entering his office, she stopped at his assistant's desk and the woman looked up. "Yes,"

"I need to see Mr. Scott."

"Your name?"

"Laurel Malone."

"Yes, Miss Malone. He said you might be here to see him. Go right in."

She opened the polished oak doors and entered his office. Mr. Scott sat behind an ornate desk purusing paperwork in front of him. His laptop was to the side up and running.

"Laurel, I thought I'd see you again today."

"Mr. Scott. I find it necessary to quit," Laurel said, knowing in her heart this was the right thing to do.

"Laurel, don't throw your career away because your father and I had a hand in it. Please sit down…."

"I don't want to sit down. I've realized today that I don't really like accounting and it's not what I want to do with my life."

"Don't be rash. Sure, you've had a shock, but it'll pass. I do value you as an employee. I intend to use your unitedthinking model on all our corporate strategies and in all our brochures."

"You're welcome to it, but I won't be here. Thank you."

She set the letter on his desk, turned, and walked out without a backward glance.

As she left the building, she felt as if a great weight had been lifted from her shoulders. She was free now to do what had always given her the greatest pleasure. Her furniture.

From Waterford Scott, she caught a cab to the leasing office for the 27th Street storefront. After paying the money for the lease, the agent handed her the key.

Laurel wasted no time. She went home and changed and called Melanie Graham at the Met.

"Melanie, I need your help."

"What can I do Laurel."

"I need a truck. I have some furniture I need moved."

"Just tell me where."

Laurel gave her directions. "Could they leave now?"

"They're on their way."

"Thanks Melanie for everything."

"It's my pleasure. I'll see you tomorrow night."

She jumped in her SUV and headed out to Cranberry. She supervised the moving of her furniture and once it was all loaded, directed the movers to her storefront. She showed the movers exactly what pieces she wanted moved into the store, where she wanted them placed, all but four pieces—the square-backed couch with the silver circles on blue, a replica of her wavy bed design, a triangular corner chair in a deep burgundy, and a dining table inlaid with geometrical designs.

"Could you please make sure that these four pieces are placed with all the art deco furniture slated for the Malone auction tomorrow night?"

"Yes, ma'am," the mover said and he and his crew left Laurel to work in her store. She worked hard all afternoon, so that she wouldn't have to think about a pair of aching blue eyes, a tender smile, or clever hands. She wouldn't have to think about Mac and how he'd lied to her to fulfill a seduction plan dictated by her father.

All she knew was that she was now at peace with herself. She realized that she didn't have to live up to her mother's expectations or her lofty reputation. All Laurel had to be was Laurel.

LAUREL LAY AWAKE in the darkness, trying to force her mind to rest. It was useless; this would be another night she wouldn't sleep through. Rather than lying wakeful in bed for hours, she rose and got dressed in the dark. Grabbing up the bag she always kept packed for her trips to Cranberry, she went outside and got in her SUV.

She drove straight through, the digital readout of her dash clock a dark green two forty-five in the morning.

Once she got there, she made her way to her garage and opened the side door, foregoing the pleasure of lifting up the large front door and getting the full view of her workshop.

She looked at the empty space where all her pieces had been and felt that triumph rise in her again.

She turned on a lamp on the worktable and directed the beam. Although she had followed her accounting curriculum religiously in college, Laurel had taken all her electives in art and design.

She pulled the stack of designs toward her and riffled through them. She chose a simple chair with a cut-out in the back shaped like a keyhole, long and lean and infinitely a statement about form and function. Rolling up her sleeves, a calm settled over her as she started to work. One hour melted into the next until exhaustion began to make itself known through burning eyes and an aching back. Her hands stilled, and she leaned back in her chair to relieve the ache.

She stared at the form she'd created. A keyhole needs a key and Laurel knew who the key was. It was her.

She laid her head down onto the worktable and closed her eyes.

The next thing she knew, she was being shaken awake. She protested and tried to drift back to sleep.

"Laurel? Wake up, dear."

It was Mr. Hayes's voice and he sounded worried. She opened her eyes to see him standing there, Wanda anxiously looking over his shoulder. Both of them were in their night clothes.

She smiled and met Mr. Hayes's eyes. He smiled back. "Come on, dear. If anyone needed my blueberry pancakes, it's you."

Laurel found herself eating pancake after pancake and pouring her heart out to Mr. Hayes and Wanda about all that had happened.

He looked somber and glanced at Wanda before he cleared his throat and began to speak. "Do you love this man?"

Laurel felt heat infuse her and for the first time in three days she came alive.

"Yes."

"Then don't throw it away. I loved a woman once. When I found out she wasn't who I thought she was, I left. I thought she was having an affair. In my sense of betrayal and bitterness, I never gave her a chance to explain. It was only later, after the divorce I found out that she had been faithful to me. I've regretted that decision, Laurel. Don't live to regret yours, dear."

Wanda put her arms around Mr. Hayes and held him. Laurel dashed away a tear.

"I'll think about it. I just don't know how I could trust him."

"Give it a shot, honey," Wanda said.

MAC OPENED THE DOOR to his loft Monday night, feeling disoriented after being away from it for what seemed like another lifetime.

The terrible fact that Laurel wouldn't believe him cut him deep. He never would have predicted that she would think that he was in cahoots with her father. But, of course, he now saw exactly how it looked.

His insides felt shredded and there was a hole where his heart should be. For a man used to success, it felt like a complete and overwhelming defeat losing her. Even saying it to himself hurt.

"Hey, brother, what are you doing here?" Tyler asked as he snapped off the TV. He took a better look at Mac's face and swung his feet off the table, his sleepy eyes losing their glassy quality.

"What happened? Is it Mom?"

"Not Mom. Laurel found out about me before I had a chance to explain."

"Ah, Mac. I'm sorry. This is all my fault. I should have kept my big nose out of your business."

Feeling raw inside and sick at losing Laurel, Mac said, "I shouldn't have listened. But you're judgment about relationships isn't always sound."

"What is that supposed to mean?"

"It means that you won't give your own father the time of day. I can't understand why you won't at least listen to what he has to say."

"We're not talking about that. I was trying to help you, Mac. You always towed the line, but sometimes you have to break the rules to get what you want."

"Yeah? It didn't work this time, but that's my problem. I'll deal with Laurel, but you need to come to terms with your own stuff."

"Don't start on that again, Mac. I don't…."

"Just listen to what the man has to say. It won't kill you."

"How do you know how I feel? You've had a father your whole life."

"That's right, I have but if I didn't, I wouldn't throw away the opportunity to meet him."

"Easy for you to say."

"You have too much pride, Tyler. Someday, it's going to be your downfall."

"This is what I get for trying to help you? Well, screw you, Mac." Tyler grabbed his leather jacket and slammed out of Mac's loft.

The silence was deafening. He knew he'd deliberately picked a fight with Tyler because he was mad, but the blame wasn't Tyler's, it was squarely on Mac's shoulders. He'd gone through with it. He'd deceived Laurel and turned her against him. There wasn't anything he could do now.

He remembered the shock in her eyes, the betrayal. He'd found and lost the woman of his dreams. How was he going to handle that? How could he live with that?

MAC GOT TO THE OFFICE early the next morning after very little sleep. The keen sense of loss seemed tenfold as if the day somehow magnified the feeling, made it more real.

He picked up the phone to call her, but put down the receiver. What more could he say? How could he convince her that he loved her and hadn't conspired with her father? He picked up the receiver again, determined to make Laurel hear what he had to say.

He started to dial her number when he heard that hard, cold voice. "Mr. Malone wants to see you."

Dread curling in his stomach, Mac followed Lucy to Mr. Malone's office.

Mac entered. There was no warm greeting this time. Mr. Malone's lips were pinched tight. He didn't even offer Mac a seat.

"What have you done to my daughter?"

"I was told Laurel wouldn't be interested in any man who worked for you, so I didn't tell her I worked here."

"I beg your pardon," Mr. Malone sputtered, looking angry.

"I'd have told her anything. She's the most amazing person I've ever known. I'm in love with her."

"Tell me why I shouldn't fire you on the spot."

"I had a feeling that was going to happen. I'm even prepared for it. But what I'm not prepared for is losing Laurel. She's infused my life with *life*. I'm not sure you can understand that because you don't really understand your own daughter. So, losing this job is nothing, less than nothing, next to losing her. She was the one searching for something missing. She says that I gave that to her, but she's wrong, she had what she was looking for all along. I'm the one who didn't know that something was missing until I met her."

"You're right. I don't understand."

"Stop trying to protect her. She's more than capable of handling her own life. You would be proud if you could really see her like I see her. Let go of her. Let her be who she is, instead of some idea you have of who she should be and who she should be with."

"I don't need you telling me what kind of relationship I should have with my daughter. I think you should find other means of employment, Mr. Tolliver. Clear out your desk and get out of my firm."

HER MOTHER'S WING rang with activity as Christie's set up the podium and the auctioneer purused the items to be offered for sale late afternoon on Tuesday. Laurel had left Cranberry after a few hours of sleep.

Attendants set up chairs while the florist shop delivered and placed the flowers. Everything was coming to-

gether. All Laurel had to do was go home and change
into her evening wear. She was turning to go, when she
caught sight of her father, entering the wing and walking past the stacked furniture lined up in the hall. Laurel followed until he turned into a small room where the
museum had collected family and individual photos of
one of their most generous benefactresses—Anne
Wilks Malone.

Her father went to the baby grand piano and sat
down on the bench. He picked up a framed photo of
his wife and he looked down into the still image for a
moment.

Then he covered his eyes and bowed his head.
Tears gathered in Laurel's eyes. This glimpse into her
father's pain struck a chord inside her, made her realize that refusing to help with the auction had nothing at all to do with indifference and everything to
do with protection. He was still having a hard time
with her mother's death and isolating himself from
the preparations for her memorial was the only way
he knew how to protect himself from drowning in
that pain.

She understood now. His meddling was his way of
compensating for his wife's loss. She suspected that her
father had never meant for her to find out about his part
in her promotion, but Laurel was glad she had. It made
it all clear to her what path she needed to follow.

The one that led straight to her dreams.

She walked into the room and sat down next to him.

"Dad," she said softly. He raised his head, rubbed his
eyes and she put her arm around him.

"I'm sorry about not participating in the memorial,

Laurel, but it's been very difficult for me. I miss her very much."

"I know, Dad. I understand."

"Good."

"Dad, I quit my job."

He set her mother's picture down and turned toward her. "What for?"

"It didn't make me happy."

"Laurel, I thought you loved accounting."

"No, not really. I only took it as a major because it's what you and Mom wanted. I would have preferred to study furniture design."

"No kidding? Why didn't you say anything?"

"Mom drilled it into me from the time I was young that I must always conduct myself like a lady. It didn't occur to me to assert myself."

"Oh, Laurel, she wouldn't have wanted you to be unhappy."

"I realize that now."

"So this is what Tolliver was talking about right before I fired him."

"What? You fired Mac. Why?"

"He was lying to my baby girl. I don't want that kind of man on my team."

"So you didn't put him up to this disguise he used to get into my good graces?"

"Of course not, Laurel, but I can understand why you jumped to that conclusion after learning what I'd done in your professional life. I am sorry."

"No, Dad, he wasn't lying to me. He was the best thing that ever happened to me. I love him very much.

"Love is precious, Laurel," her father said looking

at the picture of his wife again. "You shouldn't throw it away."

Laurel leaned over and kissed her father on the cheek.

MAC STOOD IN THE BACK of the rotunda as people bid on the art deco furniture offered in each lot. He'd debated about whether or not to come, but the truth was he couldn't stay away. Laurel was sitting up front with her father, her attention riveted to the auctioneer.

He slipped his hands into the pants of the impeccable tux he wore and although he enjoyed dressing up and doing the society thing, he had embraced the other wilder side of himself. He'd kept the Ducati that Tyler had loaned him.

Even losing his job hadn't affected him that much. He could work with his brother or go to work for his father. It didn't matter. He had plenty in the bank to hold him over until he decided what it was he wanted to do.

The only thing he regretted about pretending to be a bad-boy biker was losing Laurel.

"Ladies and gentlemen we have an addition of four pieces donated by the daughter of the late Anne Wilks Malone. Laurel Malone is both designer and craftsperson for these pieces being offered," the auctioneer said.

Mac smiled to himself. He was so proud of her, he wished he could kiss her.

He stood there watching as each piece received furious bids and added a nice amount to the museum's coffers.

When the auction ended, Mac turned and left.

LAUREL KNOCKED ON Mac's door early Wednesday morning. She hadn't been able to come last night as her duties were to her family, but now that the auction was over and her mother had received a fitting memorial, Laurel needed to right a wrong. Mac hadn't been part of a scheme her father cooked up. He'd been as original as he'd said.

It made her feel giddy that he'd gone to such lengths to meet her. Giddy and flattered.

When the door opened, Tyler was standing there.

"What do you want?" he said with unfriendly eyes.

"I need to talk to Mac."

"Haven't you hurt him enough?"

"I know and I'm sorry. Please, Tyler, give me a chance to make it up to him. I love him so much I can't bear the thought of being without him."

Tyler's eyes softened and Laurel started to hope.

"All right. He's miserable without you, too. Let me get my coat."

"Tyler?"

"Yes."

"Would we have time to stop by Hayes Cycles?

Tyler grinned and nodded. "Sure. It's on the way."

MAC HEARD THE HARD knocking all the way to his bathroom. He'd been staring in the mirror, deciding if he wanted to shave. Deciding if he wanted to go to the corner market and get the paper. He should really look for a job.

Halfway to the door the knock came again and he called out, "Hold your damn horses." The knocking only got more persistent. "I said," he pulled open the door.

"Hold your horses. I know. I heard you bellow through the door."

Laurel walked past him without a by your leave. "You can get the chair in the hall. It was a bitch lugging it up here."

Sure enough, the lipstick-red lip chair sat in the hallway.

She looked around his apartment. "This is very nice. You really do have good taste, unlike your brother."

"Decorating is not his strong suit," Mac muttered as he picked up the chair and moved it inside his loft.

"It'll fit perfectly right here."

"That's exactly what I was thinking when I first saw it," Mac said.

"I love your loft."

He was grumpy and dammit he was still hurt. Having her in his loft, so close to him only sent that aching, gnawing hunger through him. "Could you tell me what's going on?"

She smiled, a beautiful radiant smile filled with certainty. "I owe you an apology, a couple really."

Something tight and unyielding seemed to loosen around his heart. "You owe me an apology? I'm listening."

"Thank you. It's more than I allowed you."

"Go on."

She took a deep breath. "I've spent my whole life letting my father and mother do everything for me. It wasn't apathy really, it was mostly fear of taking a risk. I have no room to talk about deception since I was as bad as you. I was lying by omission to my family and friends, and that makes me a bigger deceiver then you could ever think of being. You did it because you wanted to get close to me and felt that it was the only way to do that. I did it to protect myself. I'm sorry for the cruel things I said."

He remained quiet, listening, waiting for her to continue and finish, but he liked what he heard so far. Laurel stepped closer, but didn't touch him.

"I found that the more I got to know you, the more I wanted to take a risk, on myself, on you," she said huskily. "You are the only person that I was able to confide in about what I really love to do because I trusted you on an instinctive level. I knew in my heart that you would never deliberately hurt me. It was scary how much you understood me, how much we were in tune. And you're surely no bad boy. You're trustworthy and reliable and oh-so-sexy." She smiled, a fine sheen of tears glossing her eyes. "It's quite a wonderful combination."

He trailed his fingers down her soft cheek, needing to feel her skin beneath his fingertips. "Laurel—"

She held up her hand. "Wait, I'm not done yet." She inhaled deeply, and went on. "I've been so completely selfish and so blind when it comes to what I want and need. It's true. I probably wouldn't have given you the time of day because you worked for my father and that was wrong of me. Narrow-minded. Especially when you risked everything for me...like getting fired. For that I'm deeply sorry."

"I learned something very important from you, too."

"What?" she asked.

"I learned that I liked being bad every once in a while, especially in bed. It made me take a look at my life. I wasn't experiencing life until I met you."

"Looks like we both won big." She smiled and took his hand. "I've got something to show you outside."

"I'm more interested in what I can show you right here, right now."

"Okay, I'm easy. How about you look out the window?"

He obliged her by doing so. He moved the curtains aside and started chuckling.

"How the heck did you get that chair over here on that little red Ducati?"

"Your brother drove it. He went back in my SUV."

Mac laughed. "You need a motorcycle license, you know."

"I know, but I figure I could get lessons from my bad-boy boyfriend."

"Boyfriend? I don't think so." He smiled, his chest filling up with more joy than he could hold. "It has to be more than that Laurel because I can't live without you. I'm crazy in love with you, in case you haven't figured it out. It must be marriage."

She launched herself into his arms. Her mouth was soft and warm beneath his.

"Is that a yes?" he breathed against her mouth.

"Yes, yes, yes and yes again. I love you, too."

Epilogue

Thank you for constructing your wonderful
Who's Your Hottie? *quiz. I'm thanking you because after careful reflection, I believe that a man
can't be pigeonholed into categories. Men are as
unique as fingerprints and as wonderful as the
stars. I've found my hottie, a man who embodies
all the traits I love, compassion, sense of humor,
intelligence, oh and a hot, gorgeous bod. I didn't
say I was totally altruistic. Once again, thanks for
the eye opener and the test. I think I passed with
flying colors.*

Laurel M from New York
—Letter to the editor of SPICE *magazine*

LAUREL'S STORE WAS PACKED with people and she was
beginning to believe that her Fun and Funktion Furniture was quite a hit.

The *Village Voice* was even running a piece about the
store next week. It had been a wonderful six months.
She and Mac had been married in the beautiful living
room that overlooked the ocean at Mac's parents' home
in the Hamptons.

Mac had started working full-time with his brother,

and was helping her on her busy weekends and attending to all the financial headaches of both businesses before he decided what it was he wanted to do with his life.

She rang up a three thousand dollar order for her Wavy bed design, one of her hottest sellers for the Christmas season.

"Hey there," Mac said from the doorway.

"Hey yourself," Laurel said, giving the receipt to the customer, her last one of the day. She walked toward him and wrapped her arms around his waist.

"Tyler called me just a few minutes ago. He's going to Cranberry."

"To meet his father? That's great, Mac. Mr. Hayes will be so happy to see his son again."

"That was a good idea that you had to give Tyler Mr. Hayes's e-mail address, so that Tyler could converse with him before he finally met him."

"After you told me, I couldn't rest until they met."

"I love you, Laurel."

"I love you, too."

Laurel looked up into Mac's gorgeous blue eyes and smiled. Out of the corner of her eye, she saw a black Mercedes pull up to the curb and her father got out from behind the wheel.

"Oh, my God, it's my father!"

Her father hadn't quite embraced Laurel's hobby and she'd been disappointed when he hadn't shown up to her grand opening any day since.

For a moment, her father stood on the sidewalk taking in her store. On display were the cheery Christmas lights and handmade funky reindeer and Santa Claus, the blue snowmen, and wire Christmas trees, along with the arrangement of her most popular furniture designs.

Her eyes met her father's through the glass and she saw his vulnerability. Her heart filled with love for him as he took the steps that brought him through her front door. She left Mac's arms and rushed up to him, giving him a big hug.

0805/024/MB135

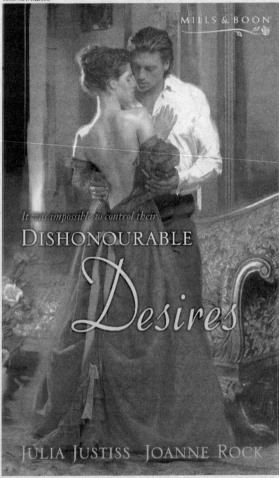

MILLS & BOON

It was impossible to control their

DISHONOURABLE

Desires

JULIA JUSTISS   JOANNE ROCK

On sale 5th August 2005

Available at most branches of WHSmith, Tesco, ASDA, Martins,
Borders, Eason, Sainsbury's and all good paperback bookshops.

Desert
Heat

Susan Mallery
Alexandra Sellers

On sale 19th August 2005

Available at most branches of WHSmith, Tesco, ASDA, Martins,
Borders, Eason, Sainsbury's and all good paperback bookshops.

0705/51

SILHOUETTE®

Desire™ 2 in 1

The **SONS OF THE DESERT**
series by **Alexandra Sellers**
new titles

SHEIKH'S CASTAWAY

and

**THE ICE MAIDEN'S
SHEIKH**

are as rich, passionate and exotic as
anyone could desire.

ALSO AVAILABLE NEXT MONTH:

ENTANGLED WITH A TEXAN by Sara Orwig

and

LOCKED UP WITH A LAWMAN by Laura Wright

(The Millionaire's Club)

BEYOND CONTROL by Bronwyn Jameson

and

VERY PRIVATE DUTY by Rochelle Alers

On sale 15th July 2005

Visit our website at www.silhouette.co.uk

*Available at most branches of WHSmith, Tesco, ASDA, Martins,
Borders, Eason, Sainsbury's and most good paperback bookshops.*

2 FREE

BOOKS AND A SURPRISE GIFT!

We would like to take this opportunity to thank you for reading this Mills & Boon® book by offering you the chance to take TWO more specially selected titles from the Blaze™ series absolutely FREE! We're also making this offer to introduce you to the benefits of the Reader Service™—

★ **FREE home delivery**
★ **FREE gifts and competitions**
★ **FREE monthly Newsletter**
★ **Exclusive Reader Service offers**
★ **Books available before they're in the shops**

Accepting these FREE books and gift places you under no obligation to buy, you may cancel at any time, even after receiving your free shipment. Simply complete your details below and return the entire page to the address below. You don't even need a stamp!

YES! Please send me 2 free Blaze books and a surprise gift. I understand that unless you hear from me, I will receive 4 superb new titles every month for just £3.05 each, postage and packing free. I am under no obligation to purchase any books and may cancel my subscription at any time. The free books and gift will be mine to keep in any case.

K5ZED

Ms/Mrs/Miss/Mr ....Initials ....
BLOCK CAPITALS PLEASE

Surname ....

Address ....

....

....Postcode................................

Send this whole page to:
UK: FREEPOST CN81, Croydon, CR9 3WZ